TEGO ARCANA DEI

Keeping God's Secret

Andrew Man

authorHOUSE®

AuthorHouse™ UK Ltd.
500 Avebury Boulevard
Central Milton Keynes, MK9 2BE
www.authorhouse.co.uk
Phone: 08001974150

First published by AuthorHouse   05/6/2011

ISBN: 978-1-4567-7987-0 (sc)
ISBN: 978-1-4567-7988-7 (hc)
ISBN: 978-1-4567-7989-4 (e)

Author's note to this new revised edition:

Following the first publication of the book last year, this new revised version includes more details of God's Secret, in order to support and enhance unexplained mysteries in the conclusion. Nothing has been removed from the original plot, just new facts added to help the reader understand the story that governments, church, and your bank do not want you to read! Any people depicted in stock imagery provided by Thinkstock are models, and such images are being used for illustrative purposes only.

Certain stock imagery © Thinkstock.

This book is printed on acid-free paper.

Good Reading

David.

**For my wife and family, with
thanks to all who have inspired me.**

Contents

Prologue — The FairyMaiden

CONNLA of the Fiery Hair was son of Conn of the Hundred Fights. One day as he stood by the side of his father on the height of USNA, he saw a maiden clad in strange attire coming towards him.

'Whence comest thou, maiden?' said Connla.

'I come from the Plains of the Ever Living,' she said, 'there where there is neither death nor sin. There we keep holiday always, nor need we help from any in our joy. And in all our pleasure we have no strife. And because we have our homes in the round green hills, men call us the Hill Folk.'

The King and all with him wondered much to hear a voice when they saw no one. For save Connla alone, none saw the Fairy Maiden. 'To whom art thou talking, my son?' said Conn the King. Then the Maiden answered, 'Connla speaks to a young, fair maid, whom neither death nor old age awaits. I love Connla, and now I call him away to the Plains of Pleasure. Oh, come with me, Connla of the Fiery Hair, ruddy as the dawn with thy tawny skin. A fairy crown awaits thee to grace thy comely face and royal form. Come and never shall thy comeliness fade, nor thy youth, till the last awful Day of Judgment.'

The King in fear of what the maiden said, which he heard though could not see her, called aloud to his Druid, Coran by name. 'Oh Coran of the many spells,' he said 'and of cunning magic, I call upon thy aid. A task is upon me too great for all my skill and wit, greater than any laid upon me. A Maiden unseen has met us, and by her power would take from me my dear, my comely son. If thou help not, he will be taken from thy king by woman's wiles and witchery.'

But as the Druid stood forth and chanted his spells, she threw an apple to Connla. For a whole month from that day, Connla would take nothing, either to eat or to drink, save only from that apple. But as he ate it grew again and always kept whole. And all the while there grew within him a mighty yearning and longing after the maiden he had seen.

But when the last day of the month of waiting came, Connla stood by the side of the King on the Plain of Judgment, and again he saw the maiden come towards him, and again she spoke to him. Then Conn the King observed that since the maiden came Connla his son spoke to none that spake to him. 'Summon swift my Druid Coran, for I see she has again this day the power of speech.' Then the maiden said: 'Oh, mighty Conn, fighter of a hundred fights, the Druid's power is little loved; it has little honour in the mighty land, peopled with so many of the upright.' 'Tis hard upon me,' then said Connla 'But yet a longing seizes me for the maiden.'

When the maiden heard this, she answered and said: 'The Ocean is not as strong as the waves of thy longing. Come with me in my gleaming crystal canoe. There is, too, another land worthy of thy journey, a land joyous to all that seek it. Only wives and maidens dwell there. If thou wilt, we can seek it and live there alone together in joy.'

Celtic Fairy Tales
Joseph Jacobs 1892

Introduction—New Life

Geneva, Switzerland— Wednesday 13 January 2010

This collection of thoughts and deeds was confused at the time, after a heart operation.

'Non, non, non,' was what he overheard in the intensive care unit at the University Hospital of Geneva. He had awakened there after having heart surgery the previous day and still felt a lot of pain. Half an hour later, a woman doctor approached his bed and spoke to him in English, 'They want to move you to my small unit—the *salle de réveil*quite close to here, all right? There is a rugby match tonight, and it may get busy in here. Don't worry. We are going to take good care of you.' After major surgery, and waking to find himself connected to an array of drips and machines, he had little choice about what happened next. This was an important Swiss state hospital, with some of the best heart surgeons in Europe. As a baby boomer, he just did as he was told.

Later that afternoon, the drips were reconnected to a mobile unit and the bed moved out of the intensive care unit into the passageway outside, where another bed was waiting. He pointed to the empty bed. 'And just how do I move across to that—fly?' he asked the gaggle of female nurses waiting to help with the transfer. After the operation, which had taken place the day before, he had no energy to argue. Besides, he had always believed that, if change was going to happen, there must be reason. He had learned that it's so much better to go with the flow and wait and see the reason later. A group of young beasts heaved him across to the next bed, a nurse attached the mobile unit to the foot of the bed, and the little convoy set off down the wooden passageways in the direction of the salle de réveil.

As they rounded the final corner, he could see that the mobile unit had disconnected itself from the steel bed. As the uneven wooden floor caused the bed to jostle on its journey, he could also see that

1

the whole unit was going to fall over. By pure chance, one of the regular hospital orderlies caught the machine just before it could crash to the ground. He looked surprised that the red locking bars had not been engaged to ensure a secure connection to the steel frame. *Just what is wrong with this generation today?*thought the patient. After that, they continued until the doors to the unit opened, signalling their arrival. Wondering what was in store, he was greeted by the same woman doctor whom he had seen before, and the team set about transferring all the drips again. As the nurses worked, the doctor apologised for the inconvenience of the transfer and asked where his black bag was. 'Upstairs in my private room locked in the cupboard,' he answered.

She nodded knowingly, 'Don't tell me, let me guess. The key is hidden in your glasses case! You British don't change a bit, do you? We will send someone up to retrieve it,' she said. They smiled at each other, at this personal understanding.

He thought to himself that it had been over five hundred years since the English virgin queen had financed the building of the walls of Geneva to help keep the town Protestant. By 1796, George Washington had made his famous speech. About the domination of one faction over another, he had said: The 'disorders and miseries which result gradually incline the minds of men to seek security and repose in the absolute power of an individual.' It had taken the World War II generation to fight against that tyranny, restore democracy, and rebuild Europe. By the time the baby boomers arrived in the UK and he walked to school in the cold winters, he wore only a raincoat and scarf over blazer and shorts. *We were all once incredibly 'green' of necessity*, he thought. It was amazing to think how little energy was used. No TV in those days, and no fridge ... a gas washing machine and no boiler when he was born. It was just a question of getting the nutty slack in the hod up from the cellar, because most heating in those days was from coal fires. Food rationing of course went on into the 1950s—no chance of being anything but fit. But where had all this gone in the twenty-first century? As he looked around the ward, everyone appeared to be from the next generation. There was a young, overweight man in the corner, maybe recovering from his first coronary attack, he wasn't sure. The salle de réveil was used to help those who collapsed in the street and were brought in by the police. In the next bed was a young woman in her early twenties, about whom he heard the nurses mention words like *dancer* and *drug overdose*. The kids today were killing themselves with a diet of fast food, hard alcohol, drugs, and little or no exercise.

Around four in the afternoon, his assistant surgeon visited him to replace the large plaster covering his heart. He watched suspiciously as the surgeon cut away the drain tubes and finally exposed the stitching. There underneath was an array of colours that he knew he had seen before. Of course, that was impossible, unless his spirit had moved outside his body in the operating theatre and had not yet returned. His mind jumped to the Tibetan Book of the Dead and tried to remember how long the spirit would remain close to the body. Just as quickly, he closed that in his mind, knowing one must exclude all negative thoughts if one doesn't want them to happen. Shortly after the surgeon had finished his work and left, another bed arrived in the ward. At first it looked to be another male casualty of cardio arrest, as the bed was placed on the opposite wall to his. Then he saw the person was an Indian with a black beard. He was still wearing a black coat. The patient not only knew this person, but had met him on several occasions before. His mind raced in a panic as the alarm sounded off on his monitor, which brought a nurse running with a top-up injection for low blood pressure. It was going to be a long and painful night.

Before he went to sleep, the nurse had bought the breathing mask and helped him settle down for the night. The air being pumped into his face felt cold as he drifted in and out of consciousness. He dreamt he was on a sailing boat at night, with the wind blowing in his face. The sky was a dark black, not really a colour but more of a huge void. There were no stars in this place to guide lost souls. By midnight, his blood pressure was down over thirty points, and the alarm on the monitor was bleeping all the time. Desperate times need urgent measures, so he took three deep breathes, and the monitor dropped one point. Two hours and three hundred breathes later, the level had returned to zero, but he was exhausted and could keep it up no longer. The large Indian opposite started to snore, and then an astral shape rose from his bed and crossed the room to rest close by the patient's bed. Had he been conscious, he would have seen a hand reach out to the monitor. As the hand touched the red numbers, the screen turned blue. The astral shape drifted away back to the other side of the ward and disappeared.

When the patient woke in the morning, the Indian and his bed were gone. Maybe it had all been a dream, but there on the floor was scrap of paper. When the nurse handed it to him, he saw it was headed in French 'Directive en Advance' with some handwritten notes below. They appeared to be advice in case of serious sickness or accident, giving wishes for medical care—number of times to be resuscitated and an agreement to turn off machines if 80 percent of body functions should fail. He thought this was some kind of a joke until he turned the paper over and saw the card was issued by Carte Federal—2012. It looked as if the population was not going to be allowed to vote on this; it would simply be introduced by the federal government.

When the doctor did his rounds in the morning, he expressed surprise at the progress his patient had made and asked what his profession was. The patient simply said he was writing a novel and that it would probably be 'an inconvenient book'. At last he was told he would return to his room at midday, and the same procedure as last time was followed for the machines. His wife was waiting outside and followed as the procession made its way back to the *sector privé*. His room on the ninth floor was about the size of a first-class cabin on a passenger ship, but with a much higher deck head. It was clean, functional, and fit for purpose, with a view of the Geneva suburbs sprawling away to the north, to the Jura Mountains. Four young nurses fussed around with the drips and changed his bed, while his wife opened some cut flowers. He was back in his room, but still did not feel right. Whilst he waited, he felt well enough to walk a few paces outside in the corridor as if looking for something. When he came back in, his wife had arranged a vase of red and yellow tulips, which he found attractive, but he had no idea why. He asked his wife why she had bought tulips instead of other flowers. 'They are part of the force of life,' she said. He knew that his heart, apart from being an efficient pump, was primarily an organ of intelligence, just like the brain. In fact, the heart emits electromagnetic energy in a range that extends over ten feet from the body. So what was happening to him now? Then he remembered someone had told him that the DNA of a tulip bulb is 70 per cent the same as the DNA of a human, but how was that possible? He could feel the flowers in the room transmitting life energy, and then it hit him. His astral body was at last returning to his physical body. He was back at last.

Feeling better, but tired, he finally slipped into bed, in need of a big sleep. *We seem to have lost perspective on what it means to be a leader,* he thought, *since the crash of 2008.* He was dreaming that it was the very politicians responsible for saving us that had brought on the crisis in the first place. He had seen creeping socialism kill his country twice in the last forty years, and now this new brand of socialism, with a smile, had taken over at home, with disastrous results. What really worried him was that Big Government was no longer seen as a dangerous animal, but as the solution to all our problems. He needed to go back in his life and see where it had gone wrong in the last millennium.

Perhaps the best place to start was down at the London docks in 1967.

Chapter 1—Early Days

The underground roads
Are, as the dead prefer them,
Always tortuous. —W.H. Auden

James Pollack was born in Devon, just after the war, and therefore qualified as one of the UK's baby boomers. He had little idea at the time that he bore the same name as one of the great American founding fathers, who had coined the phrase 'God Our Trust,' which would later appeared on all U.S. coinage revised to 'In God we trust'. James saw the end of food rationing in the UK at a time when the people were told they had never had it so good. His main hobby was messing around in boats, which he loved so much that he joined the merchant navy when he was just seventeen. He spent seven years as a navigating officer travelling around the world. Family values meant a lot to him, and at that time, all a middle-class man needed was a profession and a good wife to succeed. With his past navigating skills, he could often find his way around by just looking at the sun, hills, and other landmarks.

SS Arcadia, Tilbury Docks, England—Friday, 7 July 1967

After a three-year apprenticeship, James gained his first sea-going certificate and joined a P&O passenger liner as a junior fourth officer. He was very excited to have been appointed to one of the larger passenger ships of the P&O fleet, with a gross tonnage of 29,871. That appointment gave James the chance to sail on a line voyage to Australia. The *SS Arcadia* had been built by John Brown & Co. at Clyde bank near Glasgow and was launched in May 1953. Since then, she had received a full air-conditioning refit in 1959 and operated on the UK-Australia passenger service. He had travelled up to London by train and taken a taxi from St. Pancras railway station to the London docks at Tilbury, on the Thames estuary. By the time the taxi arrived at the quayside, passenger baggage was already being loaded. Embarkation for the passengers would not start until the afternoon, by two gangways. One gangway, at the front of the ship, was for first-class passengers, and the other, down by the stern, for crew and tourist-class passengers. The ship was dressed overall with coloured flags, and the 'P' flag was visible, indicating that the ship was due to sail later that day. James could see a crane loading cargo into the hold at the front of the ship, and another probably loading stores, into a central hold. The scene was one of intense bustle, as the ship prepared to leave for a three-month voyage away from the UK.

James asked the London cab to stop by the forward gangway, and he climbed out to survey the scene. An Indian seaman with a red turban and grey bristles approached him. 'Welcome, *saab*,' he said, saluting him at the same time. James was accustomed to working with Indian seamen from his time on the company's cargo ships, but as a cadet, he had never been saluted. The seaman helped to offload his sea trunk and a suitcase from the cab. A Goanese steward was summoned from the ship to carry his baggage on board. James was just about to mount the gangway when an army truck arrived on the quay. A sergeant and four soldiers, armed with rifles, got out and stationed themselves around the lorry. The army sergeant approached James to ask if he was the officer on duty. They had brought a valuable cargo from the Royal Mint to be loaded onto the ship. James quickly swung into action. He ran up the gangway, gave orders to the petty officer to have his luggage taken up to his cabin, and demanded who was the officer of the watch. He was just twenty years old and had become an officer in the merchant navy.

On departure days, all the officers were on duty all the time to prepare the ship for sea. James, as a junior officer, reported to the chief officer, and was quickly detailed to supervise the loading of the cargo of bullion. He had done this many times before with all kinds of valuable cargo and didn't like the work. However, company insurance terms required that an officer be present to check the loading and discharge of all bullion. This required descending into the depths of one of the cargo holds to count and supervise the stowage of the precious metal in a special lockup room where valuable cargo was stored. James was given the key to the locker room in the number two cargo hold and was told to take one of the armed soldiers with him. 'Shouldn't be any problems, but be careful with the London Dockers. Make sure the door is secured when you finish,' demanded the chief officer. James returned to the embarkation deck to meet up with the soldier and, being new to the ship, took a Lascar seaman with him to show them the way to the forward hold. First they went down a deck to the crew's quarters and followed a narrow passageway up to a bulkhead door marked 'No Admittance'. James inserted the key in the padlock, and the seaman opened the door to the cargo hold. At first the hold was dark and smelt of stale air, but on finding the light switch, James could see they were standing at the level of the lower 'tween deck'. There were wooden covers over the cargo hold below. All around were lockup rooms, mostly with refrigeration, but two were for valuable cargo. As James unlocked one of the rooms, the crew opened the hatch above, and daylight streamed down into the hold. A few moments later, a crane lowered a wooden palette containing the first of the bullion, along with two Dockers to carry the gold into the secure room.

They were busy for more than two hours, checking and counting each bar of gold with the soldier, who insisted on smoking most of the time. From what James could understand, the gold was being moved from the British Treasury, near the Tower of London for export abroad. The total shipment was 1,500 ingots, which, at 12.4 kg a bar, was over 18 tonnes. *Jesus*, thought James, *they must be exporting half the reserves of the Bank of England*. Each gold bar had a stamp on it and an official number that had to be checked with the manifesto. By the time they finished, it was past two in the afternoon, lunch was over, and James had not yet been to his cabin.

When they returned to the embarkation deck, James found all the ships' officers were lined up to meet with the company directors and visiting marine staff from the head office. Navigating, radio, and engineering officers were on one side of the foyer, and the purser officers and the medical staff on the other. It had been a tradition for some time that one of the directors would meet with all the officers of a departing vessel. James was surprised to see that there were so many women officers on the ship. Woman assistant pursers (WAPs), hospital nurses, entertainment hostesses, and children's hostesses, were all lined up. He suddenly realized he was late, hot, and dirty as he blundered into this reception party. The chief officer jumped forward and pushed him into the line of the deck officers, as the company director looked James up and down. 'Good God!' he exclaimed, 'Whatever do we have here? Where, might I ask, did you purchase this uniform from?' He was examining James's trousers, which had a narrow modern cut and had been tailored at a local shop, to save on expenses. At that point, the captain, a large man with bushy eyebrows, intervened on James's behalf and offered an explanation, 'Fourth Officer Pollack here has just joined the ship and been loading gold bullion in one of the cargo holds, so he's not wearing his best uniform. May I suggest that we ask him to change and report to my cabin when we finish here? You might want to look at his cargo manifest, which may be of interest.' James nodded as the director moved on down the line. As he left in embarrassment at being incorrectly dressed, no one said a word. Still red in the face, he slowly walked past the line of women officers, and a tall girl in a blue uniform smiled at him in sympathy. *Well,* thought James, *at least I have made an impression on someone here today.*

James quickly settled into the routine on his new ship. When at sea, there were always two officers on watch on the bridge of the ship at all times, day and night, together with two Indian seamen. When away from land, steering was done by autopilot, but it was necessary to take sights of the sun and stars to fix the ship's position. As a junior officer, James was on watch with the third officer, from eight to twelve in the morning and again in the evening, which gave him the opportunity to practice his sun sights at noon and compare his results with those of the more senior officers. The ship was sailing south by now, with a short stop at Las Palmas in the Grand Canaries to let the passengers ashore and to load cheaper fuel oil than was available in Europe. After finishing his morning duties just after noon, James would eat at the officer's mess table in the first-class restaurant where he quickly made friends with many of the junior officers like him. He soon found that the girl who had smiled at him on the day of their departure often found a place next to him for lunch.

Her name was Janet Rumford ... five years older than James, a tall, attractive, short-haired brunette. They soon found they shared the same interests in history, art, and the sea. She was an assistant purser, and although most of the other girls shared a cabin on C deck, she had a single cabin on A deck, which was an unusual privilege. A large number of Dutch WAPs had been recruited for the voyage. In fact, there werea total of some seventeen different passenger nationalities on board for the voyage, most of who were emigrating to Australia on an assisted passage. Since few English girls spoke even one European language well, the company had been forced to recruit a number of Dutch girls who could answer passenger questions and any complaints in most European languages. As the ship sailed on south, down the Atlantic towards Cape Town, the male officers changed into tropical white uniforms, and the female officers into white uniform dresses. Everyone became more relaxed in the tropical heat. One afternoon after lunch, they had a discussion about the origins of the name of the ship: *Arcadia*. James thought that some passengers equated this with the land of Australia. 'Don't worry,' said Janet, 'once they arrive in Australia, that will soon disappear.' It was after two in the afternoon, and all of the other officers had now left the table. Janet sighed. Leaning back in her chair, she allowed her short skirt to ride up her thighs and continued, 'Really, James, if you want to know about Arcadia and the "Arcadian Shepherds," we can probably find a reference book in the first class library. Come to my cabin tonight, after you finish at midnight, and we can go and look together.' With that she finished her coffee and left.

James was surprised at her direct approach and sat looking at his coffee for another ten minutes before he left the table. That evening, he went on watch at eight. The ship was just south of the equator off Gabon, in west central Africa. The weather outside on the bridge was hot and humid with a following wind matching the ship's speed. After the third officer checked the ships course and speed on the chart while James kept a lookout outside, he joined James on the wing of the bridge for some fresh air. 'Evening, James. So how's life

11

with you in this tropical heat?' he ventured. They were more than a thousand miles from the African continent, and all they could see was a carpet of stars above them and the dark sea below.

James thought for a moment and then said, 'Yes, everything's great. I sunbathed this afternoon and swam in the pool, but I do have a question about our ship's name.' He turned and leaned against the rail. 'Well, actually it's about all the names of our *ships*,' went on James. 'What's the meaning of the name "Arcadia", and does it refer to something in Greek mythology?'

His senior officer laughed and replied, 'James, that's been the history of our company since 1840. These are the places we have been trading with for over a hundred years. Have you been talking to that attractive WAP at lunch by any chance? Be careful; she's the daughter of one of our directors. So, if you upset her, you could get fired.' James just looked at the waves being parted by the bow of the ship and could only think of her parted legs at lunchtime.

Nothing more was said of the incident until just before midnight when James's colleague asked James directly, 'If you want to look in the first-class library it's locked at ten every evening, but we should have a spare key here.' He turned to look in a glass case full of keys in the chartroom. Selecting the right one, he passed it to James. 'Here you go—her family has a big estate in South Africa, so you have a lot to play for. And, James, good luck.'

James took the key. He entered the weather details in the log and waited for his relief before going to his cabin below. After freshening up with a quick shower, he took the lift down to A deck and approached Janet's cabin. The door opened at once when he knocked lightly, and James held up the key to the library. She was wearing a short pleated skirt and a revealing top, with little underneath. 'James thanks for coming down. Now let's go and see what we can find in the library.' He took her hand, and they headed for the elevator to the observation deck. The library was close to the left, and no one appeared to be around. On reaching the door, James inserted the key, and they went inside. As she locked the door behind them, she said, 'Now, James, we need the reference section. We're looking for anything to do with Arcadia, the classical Arcadian shepherds, or the Latin words *et in arcadia ego*. Just see what you can find.' James had little idea what she was looking for, but could hardly take his eyes off her short skirt and long legs as she gracefully moved around, searching through the rows of books.

'No, James,' she whispered as he reached for the switch. "Don't put on the main lights. We have reading lights here on the desks. Now can you find something of interest?' She pulled a volume from a shelf. 'Look at this old book,' she said. '*Idling in Arcadia*from 1934. The idea was that there was a time when men and women lived in perfect harmony with nature and with themselves. This was rooted in classical antiquity and one of the most fertile products of the Renaissance literary and artistic imagination.' As she read from the book, she bent over one of the reading tables, holding the book under the light. James decided it was time he started some fertile imagination of his own and came up behind her. He lifted up her skirt and felt her bare skin. The sight of her slightly parted legs as she read from the book on the table was enough to heighten his growing desire for her. Added to this were the smell of her newly washed hair and the hint of their perspiration in the heat of the enclosed library. James could no more care as his emotions took over, than he could have stopped breathing. Without a word, he placed his left hand on her neck and dared to caress the skin beneath her hair. She allowed his hand to move gently down her back. She seemed to enjoy the slight massage he gave her every few seconds. He was sure she would respond to this, but she merely sighed with the apparent pleasure of the moment. Suddenly, in a move that could leave only one meaning, she parted her legs some more.

Much to James's amazement however, Janet continued to examine the book. 'Look, James, here is a picture of Poussin's first version of the painting of the *Arcadian Shepherds*, which is now in Chatsworth House in England. See the overgrown tomb? And they are reading the inscription. The shepherdess is standing at the left and is posed in a sexually suggestive fashion, with her dress open and raised in anticipation.' James could stand it no longer. Opening his trousers,

13

he pushed forward into her. He roughly found her opening and, in an instant, her movements were harmonious with his. When they had finished and their coupling was complete, she turned and finally kissed him. 'Thanks,' she said softly. 'I really needed that. It's been a long time.' But she then went on again as if nothing had happened. 'Another interpretation of the painting is that death's claim to rule in Arcadia is challenged by the beautiful maiden, who insists she was found in Arcadia too and so is a ruler as well.' James thought he was not going to argue with her on that point, if he could just get her to slow down, but still she didn't stop. Now she was looking at a photograph of an engraving on an English estate, called the *Shepherd's Monument.* The wording was the same—'et in arcadia ego'—but the figures were clearly in different positions. Someone had proposed there was an anagram for this, which roughly translates in English as 'I Keep Gods secrets'.On saying this, she turned to James with her breasts exposed and her skirt up around her waist. She whispered in his ear, 'Are you able to keep God's secrets, James?' It was as if all time had stopped.

Cape Town,South Africa—20 July 1967

By the time James went on watch the next morning, most of his fellow officers appeared to know about his new girlfriend. James was surprised that many people who had avoided him before now smiled and asked how he was settling in on the *Arcadia*. At the usual sun sights taken at noon, one of the senior officers offered to help James with the math's for his astro-navigation and advised him; 'Look, James, you have to be more careful with the variation of the sun's declination. It's usually around 23.5 degrees, but does vary with latitude, so you need to check in the nautical almanac every day.' James was beginning to understand that, even on a ship; it's not what you know, but who you know that counts. For many of the officers, this was the first time they had sailed around the Cape to Australia. James had spent the last three years sailing to India and the Far East through the Suez Canal. Now it was necessary to take the longer route around Africa because of the recent Middle East war. Everyone on the ship knew that following the Six-Day War the previous month, the waterway had been closed and the whole region had been plunged into a war. The route around the Cape was longer and used more fuel, but no ship owner was going to risk a passenger ship in a war zone.

As the ship approached South Africa, the passengers started to get excited about going ashore. Many shore excursions had been planned for them during their stay in Cape Town. Even Janet asked James at lunch the next day which car he like driving, to which he had replied a Mini, knowing that she must be booking cars for many of the passengers. On the night before arrival, she dropped a hint about coming by after midnight, but he had to refuse. With an ETA at 06.00 hours, he would need to be present in his cabin for his call to stations on their arrival.

With the ship's new fifty-mile radar, they picked up the coastline early in the morning, and by six o'clock, Table Top Mountain could be seen in front of the ship. Once they had docked and secured the ship alongside the quay, everyone went for an early breakfast. Many of the girls who were off duty were already in casual clothes, but Janet, still in uniform, looked in desperation at James. As he left the restaurant, he said in a low voice, 'Get changed. I'll call for you at your cabin as soon as I can.' And he left to request shore leave from the chief officer. By the time James knocked on the door of his superior, the chief officer was in the office with several officials. 'Excuse me, sir, but would it be possible for me to go ashore for the day?' asked James.

'Well, normally no,' replied the chief, 'but if you are needed to entertain Miss Rumford, then it would be possible. Please make sure you are back for your duties at eight p.m.' James rushed back to his cabin, changed into some casual clothes, and went down to give Janet the news.

Janet was ready in jeans and a sweater. She kissed James and announced that she had the papers for the car already. They went down the gangway and found a red Mini waiting for them on the quayside. James got in to drive and quickly looked in the glove box for a map. 'So, James, where are you taking me?' asked Janet.

'Well, I thought we would go and look at the penguins on Boulder Bay, down by the Cape, and then maybe go for a swim.' he replied.

Janet looked in amusement at him and replied, 'Yea, great idea! Drive on, James!' Fortunately, James was able to find the scenic route out of the town towards the Cape quite quickly. He really enjoyed driving the little car down to the Cape. By the time they had driven through Simons Town and onto Boulder Bay, it was cloudy and blowing a gale. 'Come on, let's go and look at the waves,' said James, realizing that it really was the middle of winter in the southern hemisphere. Reluctantly, Janet left the car and approached James. 'Look, I haven't been altogether honest with you either. My father has a house close by here, up on Mount Pleasant. What do you say we go and swim there? And, James, I think I had better drive.' Janet took the keys from James and motioned him to the passenger seat. The next moment, wheels spun sand as she reversed back onto the road. She drove up away from the coast for a short time, throwing the car around corners at maximum speed until they came to a narrow road that led up to a low house set in the hillside. A stone wall topped with wire surrounded the property, but the iron gates opened as they approached. Once inside the estate, James expected wild dogs and armed guards, but there was no one at all. Janet, looking pleased, opened her door and explained, 'Unfortunately, Daddy couldn't make it today, so we are here on our own. There is just the caretaker here with his wife to look after us, if that's okay.' And, taking his hand, she led James up the steps to the entrance to the house.

As soon as they entered the house, James realized that her family were not just rich, but loaded—and this was just their summerhouse by the coast. The small entrance opened out onto a full-sized swimming pool, with glass windows all around. Janet apologized, 'Sorry, James, but there was no time to heat the pool. We can use the Jacuzzi next to it, which should be great!' James could see a secluded area in a corner, partitioned by bamboo screens and potted plants, where couples could be discrete together. 'Excellent idea,' he said as Janet used the phone to order some lunch for the two of them. 'How about lobster salad and some white wine from the estate?' she offered, to which James just nodded. While James was in charge of her on the ship, it was clear that Janet would take charge of James on the land. She strode forward to the Jacuzzi, stripping off her clothes with abandon. 'No need to be shy here, James. We are on our own, and the water should be over 30 degrees Celsius, which is better than the water temperature down at your beach!' James followed her to the Jacuzzi and removed his clothes. When he had carefully folded them and laid them on a wicker chair, he joined her in the warm water.

After some twenty minutes, the caretaker and his wife arrived with a silver trolley piled high with seafood and fruit. In a silver bucket was a bottle of white wine. When they were alone again, James pulled himself away from a wet embrace and fetched a glass for each of them. Janet was already excited, and her face was glowing pink with passion. She finally accepted a towel from James and climbed out of their hot pool. They served themselves lunch on a bamboo table, with Janet sitting on James's knee and feeding him lobster. Finally, James insisted she sit down and behave herself, to which she just drank more of her family's excellent Cape wine! 'Look, my dear,' said James teasing her, 'how can you possibly condone this lifestyle that embraces the seven deadly sins, which include things like lust and greed?'

Janet smiled and then laughed at him, 'James, first, the seven deadly sins are not in the Bible. They were written by Dante some four hundred years ago to control the peasants, if I remember correctly, so they have little to do with us today, all right?'

James looked at her in awe. 'How do you know about all these things? I mean the *Shepherds Monument* and all that stuff you talked about?'

Janet looked at him for a moment and then replied, 'If you are a good boy, I will show you one of God's little secrets we have here. Later on, okay? Right now, I'm going to have a body massage.' She nodded to her manservant, who was waiting behind a bamboo screen.

James was becoming used to her decadence. He wasn't surprised as the two servants pulled out a large massage table and placed it close to the pool. 'Come on, James, don't be shy. You don't need a towel or anything for this.' And she climbed onto the table completely naked. The two servants appeared used to such behaviour, and the man started to pour oil onto Janet's back. James reluctantly left his lunch and climbed onto the massage table beside the girl. The woman servant poured oil onto his back and started to massage his body as well. After some time, Janet turned her head and reached out with an arm for James. He had to admit she looked stunning, with her long legs all covered in oil, and her hair more red than brown. From her smile, he knew she wanted much more. When he gave her his hand, she placed his fingers in her mouth and sighed as her masseur pleasured her some more. After the massage, the two servants withdrew and she pulled James towards her with some force. By now James was also aroused. He got up and stood at the end of the table, then flipped her onto her back, pulling her legs above him. She stared at James in anticipation. In defiance, he played with her for a moment and then forced his way deep into her. As they moved together, she sat up and placed her arms around his neck, with her eyes extended in deep concentration. Still inside her, James placed his hands under her bottom and lifted her up against him. As he stood with her legs wrapped around his back, they quickly came together. James staggered back, and still entwined, they fell together into the swimming pool behind them.

Janet was the first to surface from the cold water and was laughing with joy. 'James, that was terrific! Now I will show you one of our little secrets downstairs.' She quickly called her servants to bring bathrobes, as James swam to the ladder to help her out. 'Having ruined my hair, I will need a while to get back into shape. So, dear James, finish your lunch, and I'll join you shortly.' After that, James was delighted to be alone, and returned to the wine and delicacies on the table. Finally, he freshened up with a hot shower and put on his shorts and shirt again. By the time he was finished, Janet returned dressed in shortshorts and a sleeveless orange top. Taking his hand, she led him away from the pool to a staircase that descended to the level below. First she turned on the lights and then raised the steel shutters to expose a view of the coast and the ocean outside. James looked at the scene below, but he then saw that the whole room was an enormous library, with two walls full of books. In the centre was a billiard table, and at one end, two reading tables for study. As James approached the books, he could see that each volume was bound in leather and must be worth thousands of pounds. 'So, James, what do you think? This is where we keep all our treasures—except one of course.' James was becoming confused at all the surprises, but turned to look at where Janet was pointing. In a flash he saw that a replica of the *Shepherd's Monument* was mounted in a corner of the wall.

'My goodness, Janet, you really are a surprise! I suppose you have known about this all your life?' he asked.

'Well, since I was about six. But come have a look, James.' And they both moved over to the corner to stand before the engraving. 'You can see in this version that the men and the woman are on different sides of the tomb—quite different from the Chatsworth painting, and a lot more serious.' She then went on, 'You see, James, Poussin has painted codes into most of his work—codes that point to certain stars in the constellations. In this scene, the woman now on the right can be associated with the constellation of Virgo. She symbolises justice and the virgin mother of Jesus. This man on his knees is Hercules, and his finger is pointing at the word *Arcadia* on the engraving. Come; let me take your hand.' When James put his hand into hers, she placed their fingers against the wall, and the monument opened up to allow their hands *inside* the solid image of the tomb. Janet quickly pulled his hand out, and the engraving resumed its solid state again. James looked at her in amazement. 'Sorry, James, you are still too young to understand all these secrets, but now that you have taught me about love, you can see that another dimension in our life may also exist.'

They returned to the ship in time for James's duties at eight that evening and remained close friends for many years. However, James knew that his role was to help Janet understand men, and because of her family's wealth, they could never marry. At the same time, she had interested James in something that he could never have imagined before ...an interest that would lead to new discoveries in his future life. Although he visited her holiday home in the Mediterranean, he was never invited again to the house near the Cape. It was, in fact, Janet who encouraged James to widen his horizons and start a new career in banking and finance. It was almost the end of the Anglo-American century. Little did James know that the next millennium was going to be a lot more dangerous and volatile?

Dartmoor, England—27 May 1983

Fifteen years later, James was driving out of Exeter fast along the A30 towards Oakhampton in Devon. The weather had been lousy, with persistent rain all day; the fields were already full of water. This was the West Country in late May. The April showers were over, and the late spring brought heavy rain to this part of southwest England.

Traffic was light at this time of the year; the roads would be blocked with holiday travellers only later in the summer. Still there were always big trucks on their way south to Plymouth and Cornwall beyond. Taking advantage of the dual carriageway, he was able to overtake some of the slower traffic. He was driving fast—too fast at times—at speeds of well over the seventy-mile-per-hour limit in the UK, but he didn't care. He had promised his mother that she would be on the moor by sunset, and he was not going to break that promise. James was of Saxon origin, with blonde hair and blue eyes. His long arms and legs were balanced by a large chest and a round face that always offered a grin. His easy appearance was not always appreciated by his bank employees. With his long arms, he was a good bowler at cricket, moving slower than most, with a strong will and lots of determination. Wearing traditional business suits and a tie, he was attractive to many of the opposite sex where he worked. Although married, he was not adverse to a little romance with his colleagues, who found his intensity and directness often led to sexual desire. At times, he was old fashioned—one of the old school tie. Although this was perhaps true, he resented such criticism.

As a happy-go-lucky sort of guy of thirty-seven years of age, he was already an experienced lover and enjoyed these discrete encounters.

As a Taurus, he had a creative streak, often expressed in an artistic way. Because he loved things of beauty, he was willing to work hard in order to have nice things and pleasant surroundings. The physical side of his life was important to him including romance, good food, music, and ballet. He even had a passion for gardening. The sign of his ascendant was Scorpio, so there was a formidable side to his character. He often had the ability to see straight through some people, as if he had known them before. He had a strong character, which was patient most of the time, with a still-waters-run-deep quality. With his positive, extravert personality, he had done well in his new career of international banking, but his old family clairvoyance was going to lead him from the past into a new age of time travel and the occult.

James's new car was a 'Triumph' of British engineering, not only in name, but in performance as well. But he was not interested in anything today except his mission. After delays in Oakhampton, he was finally on the main road, which skirted the moor. James looked up and could see this foreboding mass of granite on his left—until he came to a junction with the A306 going south to the village of Lydtor. He had not looked at the map, but felt this was right, so he followed the road south. Once in the village, he could see the moor again, shrouded in mist. He drove straight towards his destiny. There were few signs in those days, and he had been only a child when he had last visited the place. The tarmac road gave way to a dirt track, and he finally approached a gate equipped with a sheep trap to keep the animals from straying out. Now in a sweat, he drove until he reached the stream and the end of the road. Climbing out of the car, he took only the small urn with him. The rain was lifting at last, and with a few breaks in the clouds, he could see rays of sunshine, which fell on the moor a few miles away. This was a desolate place, but now he knew his way; his objective lay less than a mile away. James jumped the stream and made his way up the hill. There must have been a path, which he would find in due course, but he was keeping his eye on the setting sun. It must be done before sunset, his mother had insisted. It had been done like this for generations, and he could not afford to fail. Although the rain had stopped, the wet heather was making the legs of his trousers wet. Mist still covered the top of the tor as he started to climb towards the top.

The slabs of granite became larger and larger as he scrambled higher and higher. At last he could make out the granite cross on the summit. This was the famous Wiggery's Cross on Dartmoor, a place only visited by rabbits and a few tourists in summer. There was no one here now; just the cold wind and the wet mist. James heaved himself up onto the last boulders until he was level with the cross. Carefully taking the casket out of his pocket, he removed the cork stopper and waited. Just at that moment, the clouds parted, and a ray of sunshine fell upon the cross. The omens looked good, just as his mother had said. 'Wait until there is a sign,' she had said. Suddenly, he emptied the ashes from the urn into the wind. There was nothing more ... no crash of lightening ... nothing ... just the wind howling in his ears and a cold granite cross.

Tears of grief ran down his face, and he felt relief at keeping his promise. He knelt down and said a prayer. James was wet, cold, and very much alone, or so he thought. Having climbed straight up at the front of the cross, he thought he would climb down behind in the shelter from the wind, where there was a path. He had climbed down the first twenty feet when he saw something—or somebody—hiding in the rocks. He looked again; it was a man with a beard huddled up against the rocks in a black coat, sheltering from the wind. James said nothing. He just stared in disbelief as the man slowly turned to survey his quarry. 'So you came,' he finally said. 'You kept your mother's promise—just in time too,' he went on in a foreign accent that James did not recognize.

'Who are you?' James asked. 'And what do you know of my mother?'

'Let's just say that I am here to protect you. You will see me only when you most need my protection, where ever you go.'

'How can you be my guardian when we have never met?' James laughed. 'And, anyway, how did you know my mother?' His tone was unfriendly.

'Look,' said the man, 'there are things that happen in this world that we never talk about. Your mother knew of them all. One of the best things she knew all about was "milk for the babies and meat for the men." Seeing as her offspring are all boys, she had no choice but to call on *you*—she had no other choice.'

'Okay, so you are not the tramp I thought you were, but what exactly do you want of me?' James asked. He knew a little of his mother's obsession with tea leaves and the tarot, or her other occult interests.

'Well, that's not up to me, is it?' said the stranger. 'It really depends on what you do. The gates will be closing soon; they'll not reopen for some time. You need to find out where it'll be next time—overseas or here, that's all you have to know.' With that the man stood up and disappeared into the mist.

'Wait … wait a moment!' James cried out, but it was too late. The man was gone. James was left with little choice but to descend to his car and return to the family gathering. The job was well done, but he was reminded of the three witches in Shakespeare who say at the opening … 'Where the place?Upon the heath. There to meet with Macbeth.The mist was now swirling all around his head, and he could feel someone pulling his arm. 'James, James, you must wake up!' He could hear one of the nuns talking in his ear. Slowly he came back to consciousness, only to find he was still in the abbey chapel, where they had assembled to pray. He looked up only to see the altar with the cross, and realized he must have dozed off in one of the pews. 'The sister has come to give you some news,' was all he heard. He knew exactly what he had to do next …

City of London, England – July 1983

All of that had happened less than a year ago, and now he was working for one of the blue chip merchant banks in the City of London. He had grown tired of the big U.S. banks all wanting a piece of the action in the new London interbank market, which had grown up in the 1980s. With all the petro dollars being deposited in London, banks no longer financed just one asset, but fleets of ships or aircraft.

Little was approved by credit committees. His boss, a director of the bank, bought companies left and right, only to sell them again at a big profits. Such was the frenzy of the market at that time.

James had his mind on another kind of vessel, a long-legged French girl whom he had hired as his new assistant. He had always admired young girls who speak a foreign language and dress in European fashion, with short skirts and silk scarves. She was, of course, intelligent and had been hired for her language skills and Paris education, rather than her attractive wardrobe.

It was past six in the evening, and James was just thinking of taking her to one of the new wine bars for a bit of relaxation when his private line flashed. It could not be ignored. To his surprise, it was someone he had never heard of—a Brit who said he was calling on behalf of a wealthy businessman who was attending a conference in London. Would it be possible for James to meet this man this evening at the Intercontinental Hotel in the West End? The caller gave no names, but when James enquired about the nature of the business, the man simply told him it was for a sizeable international credit, which his superior would like the bank to consider. The man told James to come to a private suite at the hotel and to bring his passport, as they would leave that evening for Switzerland by private jet. James agreed and said he would be delighted to come to the meeting.

After clearing his desk, James left the bank and headed for the bank tube station. He wondered if this was the opportunity abroad he had been waiting for. His passport was in his jacket pocket, but his mind was on his first voyage—the one he took when he joined the navy in 1967. He was at another crossroad in his life, and he was excited about where it would all lead.

Chapter 2—The New World

Broad Street, London—Monday, 18 July 1983

My heart desires to go down to bathe myself before you,
That I may show you my beauty in a tunic of the finest royal linen...
—Egyptian poem circa The Turin Erotica Papyrus 1292–1075 BCE)

The excitement of London in the 1980s led to love and romance in unusual places ...

By July, James had received the contract to work for a bank in Geneva. He was excited at the prospect of becoming one of those world-famous Swiss bankers, with numbered accounts and other secrets. His work at this British bank was interesting, but he yearned to learn what was on offer in other European cities. He was thinking of not only culture and different languages, but also of the social life available. He had read somewhere that the ratio of women to men in Geneva was six to one, which would need some investigation.

James was at his office on a hot summer afternoon of Monday, 18 July 1983. The temperature had been over 80 degrees Fahrenheit in London, and it was too hot to do much work. The office had been a 1980 makeover of some old administrative offices, with a touch of green carpets, but no air conditioning. There were modern offices for the managers and an open-plan area for the secretaries and young assistants. It would take most of the other banks in town over ten years to catch up with such innovation. The time was 5.30 p.m., and as he looked out of his office, he saw that many of his colleagues had already left early. The holiday season had started, and as his director was already on leave in the south of France. James thought the best to do was to catch the early train home, with a stop off at his squash club for a beer. He tidied up his desk, which meant moving the papers from his out-tray back into his in-tray. His objective was to make it look as if he has lots to do, but in reality nothing would happen until his boss came back from holiday. That was still weeks away. The banks in London were making huge profits from re-lending the petro-dollars they had received from oil revenues, so a summer break was welcome in the fast-expanding world of international corporate finance.

James checked his briefcase to make sure that his work contract with the Swiss bank was still there, then he left his office went to say *au revoir* to his attractive young assistant. He had tried to interest her in some after-work relaxation, but it turned out that she was betrothed to a Latin lover in Bayswater, and she had resisted all his advances. Looking at his watch, he found it was just a quarter to six, so if he hurried he could catch the 18.05 train from Broad Street Station back to Richmond. James had been commuting on the North London Line for over three years. This railway line cut through the inner suburbs of north London, from Richmond in the west to Broad Street station in the City of London, roughly in a semicircle. Broad Street Station had been built by the Victorians in 1856 as a terminus for the commuter railways, linking east and west London. James had little knowledge of this; all he knew for sure was that it was slow, with dreadfully old rolling stock that was probably due for demolition. The alternative, however, was to take the fast train to Waterloo Station, and travel on the even more-unpleasant City Line, mobbed by thousands each rush hour and also subject to delays and lightning strikes. He preferred to sit on one train for longer and endure the many stops through the decaying landscape of urban London. In fact, the train at that time made some fifteen stops after Gunnersbury, just north of the Thames through Willesden Junction, to Hampstead Heath, Gospel Oak, Camden Road, and descending down to Highbury & Islington, before joining the link to Broad Street Station in the City. The line between Broad Street and Richmond had been electrified by theLondon and North Western Railway (LNWR) in 1916 on the fourth-rail DC system. James also had little idea of this, or what a part it would play in his life before he left London.

James hurried out of his office and down Old Broad Street in the direction of the station. The pavements were full of commuters walking towards the bigger and now more-active terminus of Liverpool Street Station. He stopped at the dual carriageway at Moorgate, smiling at the scantily clad models in a fashion shop window, and moved on towards his destination. The temperature in the summer afternoon had brought out all the young secretaries in their miniskirts and see-through blouses, which excited James even more. He loved the hot and humid smells of these girls, probably a mixture of cheap perfume and too much hair lacquer, but he felt part of this scene. This was London in the 1980s, after the time of the Beatles, but with new groups like Queen, and James loved every part of it. If only he could find someone attractive to share the long journey home, he would be delighted. He knew from past experience that all the young girls would soon disappear towards Liverpool Station, as only the older folks and foreigners lived in the north London suburbs. Climbing the stairs to the Broad Street entrance was like going back in time. He entered the concourse with its dilapidated canopy that had probably not changed since after the war in 1945. By 1983, there were only three platforms still in operation, and commuter trains ran only every half-hour during the rush hours.

James surveyed the scene of a decaying building and took in the dirty platforms and the fact that the building was home to hundreds of pigeons. There was just one old commuter train waiting at the platform, with three carriages, each with individual compartments. Each compartment had an old-fashioned door on each side of the train, with brass door handles, which turned clockwise to open. James walked down the platform looking into each compartment. The first carriage was already full of the usual tired workers going home; the second was less full, but no one young or attractive was present. He had almost given up all hope when, there in a compartment of the last carriage, was a young women who looked interesting to James. He turned the door handle to her compartment, which was otherwise empty, and sat down opposite her on the bench seat. To start with, he didn't say a word. He placed his briefcase in the luggage rack above him, took off his jacket, and laid it on the faded seat beside him. He then noticed that perspiration had soaked into his shirt under his arms, and his passenger was touching her brow with a paper tissue. Before long, they looked at each other and smiled. They shared remarks about the weather, which they agreed was altogether too hot!

James introduced himself as a banker from the National Express Bank PLC. 'One of the largest commercial banks in London,' he remarked. The girl said her name was Jessica Loeza and that she was visiting England for a week, from the United States. She had been sightseeing in and around the city all day, visiting first the Tower of London and then a number of churches in the city, which James had never heard of. 'There is just so much history to see in London,' she went on. 'You probably know that many of the British monarchs had their wives and sisters beheaded. How awful!' she exclaimed in an excited voice and held up some of the tourist publicity lying in her lap.

'So what do you do for work?' enquired James. 'Oh! I trained as a biologist and work at a research centre in New Mexico, just outside Albuquerque,' Jessica replied. 'We are looking at how plants and animals can be expected to evolve in the next ten thousand years.' She smiled at James. 'Did you know that most life on this planet shares the same genes—humans have 98 percent of the same genes as a chimpanzee and 75 per cent of the same as a giraffe.' Jessica could see that James had little knowledge of this and, knowing that it's the first impression that counts with a man, really surprised him when she said, 'In fact, we now know that 33 percent of the genes of man are the same as those in a tulipbulb!'

James pretended to be surprised. 'Oh!' teased James, 'I suppose that percentage rises to over 50 per cent in girls, which makes you smell sweet and look attractive.' Jessica started to blush, but was not sure if it was from anger or from the hint that she might be attractive to him. She could not help herself and retorted, 'It's not the genes, silly, they are just the building blocks—it's the switches that decide whether an animal or a plant has legs or fins, wings or petals, and all that sort of thing.' Looking at her, James thought it was time to change the subject and asked, 'So what else do you have in Albuquerque?'

Taken off her guard, Jessica replied, 'Oh, it's mainly scrub-land.'

And James just replied, 'Yes, that's what I thought,' as if to confirm that most of her ideas were a bit bizarre.

James started to study this woman more closely; she appeared at first to be a young girl of medium height and build with dark red hair and brown eyes. He couldn't help noticing her young breasts and her sun-tanned legs and arms. From her age, she could be one of the city dolly girls, but her clothes showed she was older and perhaps more experienced. Her clothes were clean, but looked a bit dated for the fashionable '80s. She wore a knee-length yellow skirt with a white cotton blouse edged with lace, quite old fashioned. The sandals on her feet had white straps, perhaps comfortable for walking, but looked well worn. She wore no rings or jewellery, except a small cross around her neck. By now James couldn't believe his luck as they were still alone in the compartment, and the train had already made its first scheduled stops at Canonbury and then Highbury & Islington.

He was quickly brought back from his dream when Jessica asked him about his interests in life. 'So, James, what do you do when you are not working?' she asked.

'Well,' he replied, 'I play a bit of sport, like messing about on boats. And I enjoy a good read.'

'Read anything good lately?' was her reply, at which James took down his brief case, opened it and handed her a paperback by the English author John Fowles.

'This has just been published; well last year … it's called *Mantissa*. You must have heard of Fowles. He wrote *The French Lieutenant's Woman*. They're making that book into a film.' He handed her the paperback, but she just looked at him blankly. 'Well, since you ask and know something about evolution, you might be interested to know that this novel explores reality and creativity in the relationship between men and women—the battle of sexual insult and strategy,' he went on. Now it was his turn to play the dominant male and show her that he might have some intelligence after all. He started to read out loud each review on the back cover. He hardly noticed that they were now both sitting forward on their seats opposite each other, holding the book in their hands, both aroused at the sexual description. Jessica had involuntarily allowed her knees to open, and her skirt to rise, giving James a glimpse of her long legs. James also felt something rising as they both watched the increased concentration on the other's face. Jessica was surprised at the intensity of their encounter as lines on her forehead grew and a new pink flush spread to her cheeks. James took full advantage of the situation by placing the book on the fabric of her skirt between her parted legs. Then, taking her face in his hands, he kissed her fully on the mouth.

At that moment, the train shuddered to a halt at Camden Road, and the carriage doors banged open and then banged shut again. The door opposite them in their compartment opened, and an elderly, dark-skinned woman climbed inside with several plastic shopping bags. The intrusion shattered all the intimacy James and Jessica had built up. Jessica calmly took the book in her hands, smoothed down her skirt, and started to read the novel. James's ego was crushed. He looked out at the decaying London landscape. At the next station, Kentish Town, the train stopped, and the elderly passenger got off leaving them alone again. James looked at Jessica and grinned, not certain if she was really reading the book or just being polite. Jessica looked up and remarked, 'Wow, this author is different—sex therapy for memory loss! Never studied that!' she said in her American drawl.

'Well there's a lot more,' James replied. 'It's all about the way the biological cards have fallen, freeing twentieth-century woman from her reproductive role, which lets her love every minute of her life. You should read it.' She made no verbal reply, although she could see where his line of conversation was leading and felt excited by it. She studied him closely as the train started moving again. This time, it was Jessica who put the book down on the seat beside her. She reached out for James. He moved across to her side of the compartment, and they kissed again. James pushed up her skirt to reach her underwear. At this point, James went into overdrive as they kissed on the lips. Then he sank onto his knees to caress her legs, thighs, and the space between. Jessica was now taking control as she held his head in her hands and pulled it up to rub his face against her breasts. In the hot, closed compartment she was aroused by his masculine scent, which was pushing her over the top.

Jessica was now very excited. Placing her feet on the opposite seat, she raised her hips to allow James to remove her knickers. The rough fabric of the seat on her bare bottom didn't even bother her; she was overcome by what James was doing between her legs. James stood up in the swaying carriage and stuffed the flimsy fabric of her knickers into one of his trouser pockets. The noise of the train suddenly increased as it entered a tunnel, and the compartment was plunged into sudden darkness. Seeing this opportunity, it was Jessica who pulled down his zipper, letting him free to complete his conquest. In the darkened compartment, he pulled Jessica onto her back and, with her legs in the air, plunged forward into her. What happened next was beyond James's comprehension. First there was no Jessica on the seat beneath him. Then he felt he must have passed out in his moment of passion! As the train drew into the next station at Hampstead Heath, he found himself slumped over in the corner of the compartment with his trousers down. He was brought to his senses when a man opened the door of the compartment. When he saw James's bare bum, he quickly went elsewhere. James was ashamed of his behaviour. He couldn't understand what had happened to Jessica. He quickly pulled up his trousers and rearranged his clothing in case someone should report him to the railway staff.

He thought, *she must have got off the train as it pulled into Hampstead station*. Then he noticed that the book she had been reading was missing as well. He sat down on the seat again and smiled to himself as he suddenly realized he still had her knickers in his trouser pocket. He couldn't believe what had happened. *Are all American girls that fast?* He wondered. He now had another twelve stops on the North London Line to dream about her and their brief meeting. If she was spending a week sightseeing in London, he was sure he would see her again at Broad Street Station, if only to return his book.

Gunnersbury Station, West London—Friday, 22July 1983

James spent the rest of the week looking out for Jessica on his way to and from work. He even spent a part of his lunch hour looking in some of the churches she had mentioned on the train, but there was no sign of her. He caught the same 6.05 p.m. train home each evening and checked every carriage to see if she was on the train. By Friday, the weather was still baking hot and sunny for London, with a fine haze of pollution now covering the capital. By now James had become desperate to find the girl again. His young assistant at the bank guessed that his obvious problem involved a woman, but said nothing. In the evening, James has almost given up hope, but left the office in good time to catch his usual train. He walked briskly down Broad Street overtaking most of the other commuters on their way home. When he reached the street outside the station, he saw one of those stretched American cars parked at the bottom of the stairs. A couple of policemen were standing nearby along with some press photographers.

On seeing the crowd of people waiting outside, James bounded up the stairs and entered the station concourse, where another crowd of youngsters were waiting outside a brightly painted caravan, which was also surrounded by a police cordon. This had not been there in the morning James recalled. Coloured bunting had been place all around the platforms, and billboards announced: 'Give My Regards to Broad Street' in big black letters. James wondered what was going on at his usually dull and decrepit station, which appeared to have finally joined the twentieth century. Then he realized that most of the attendees were teenage girls wearing some of the shortest miniskirts he had ever seen and some sort of pop-star T-shirts. He asked one of the girls what had been happening and she handed him a folded poster with the same words at the top and an outline of a robber below. The girl said it had been very exciting—with a film being shot at the station all day. James laughed at the news and thought it was about time someone closed this station down.

However, he was never going to find Jessica in this crowd of excited schoolgirls, so he quickly made his way to the one-and-only train waiting at the platform. On reaching the usual three carriages, he found to his dismay that the train was already full; in fact, there were people standing in each compartment. He reluctantly entered the train. The thought of standing for an hour all the way to Richmond was starting to dull his ego as he searched each compartment for a familiar face. After looking through the first two carriages, he was starting to panic. But then, in the first compartment of the last carriage— in a compartment full of standing commuters—he saw Jessica. Her face was pressed against the window, and she was waving frantically at him. He waved back and opened the carriage door, only to be glowered at by a large Indian man towering above him.

James had to push his way onto the packed train, making apologies to all, until he stood directly in front of the seated Jessica. He was just able to place his briefcase on the luggage rack and close the door as the train lurched forward and started the journey home. Jessica giggled, and as she laughed, he lowered his head to kiss her. In a flash, she had her fingers around his tie and was pulling his lips deeper into her mouth. As the train gathered speed, they were both laughing at each other. James swayed above her, and it was not long before he placed his knee between her legs to gain more support on the swaying train. Jessica clasped her knees around his leg and then reached up and took hold of his belt, while James clung on to the luggage rack. When he looked down at her, he saw she was holding one of the film posters in her lap, together with his book. With all the heat and the people in the small compartment, James thought the situation had the makings of a most promising journey home.

The train made all the usual stops though the stations of north London, and it was not until they were past Camden Road that all of the standing passengers finally left the train. When they stopped at Gospel Oak, the women sitting next to Jessica finally left her seat, and James was able to sit down next to Jessica in the corner. It was then that he realized that she was wearing the same pop-star T-shirt he had seen all the girls wearing at Broad Street. And she was wearing a white mini-skirt, which left most of her thighs exposed. He turned and whispered in her ear, 'So what exactly have you been up to today? Your clothes look a lot different from what you were wearing last time I saw you.'

Jessica smiled at him and replied that it had been an interesting day. 'When I arrived at the station about ten this morning, it was already hot, and the pollution was hurting my eyes. I went and sat on a seat at the end of the platform and read your book. After about half an hour, all the trains had left, and other people started to arrive with that caravan you saw. There was even a coffee stand with snacks. One of the railway staff came and asked if I was one of the extras, so I just said yes! Then, a bit later, two men approached me. One was young, with long hair and a round face. He said his name was Paul, although I had never seen him before. The other was fat with a moustache. I only found out later he was the film director.'

'Hang on a minute,' interrupted James, 'you were approached by Paul McCartney, an ex-Beatle, while he was making a film at Broad Street Station? That sounds crazy!'

'Okay, calm down,' she said. 'Let me tell you what happened next. This guy Paul thought a shot of me sitting on the bench at the end of the platform was really great for the film, and he asked if I would sit there while they set up the cameras. Really, James, this all happened today. I'm not making it up. So I sat there for a bit, then a makeup girl came and played with my hair, shook her head at my clothes, and went off in despair!' James looked at her quizzically. 'Yes,' she continued, 'I had the same long yellow skirt on this morning that I was wearing the last time I saw you. But that all changed, as you saw, and I thought you would like it. After a bit, I was told they had finished, and this guy Paul came and took my place. One of the film crew told me to go and get changed into the outfit that was worn by all the film extras. He said I would get a free snack at lunchtime and fifty quid—whatever that is—if I would stay on for the day, just in case they wanted a to do a re-take. I agreed and went to the women's rest room where a girl gave me this T-shirt and rather short skirt.' Jessica blushed and whispered in his ear, 'James, if I lift up this poster—you know when I'm sitting down—you can see everything as I'm not wearing any panties!'

James just laughed. 'Well, I'm not surprised about that, because they are in my briefcase!' He smiled, thinking this was becoming quite interesting. Jessica blushed at what she had said and looked so attractive with the light reflecting off her dark brown hair, the highlights shining red in the evening sunlight. Her closeness was starting to arouse James again. The problem was that there were still other passengers in their compartment. Taking off his jacket and folding it across their knees, he slowly placed his hand on Jessica's bare thigh, just below the hem of her skirt.

'James, just what do you think you are doing?' she pleaded in a low voice. James just pressed on until he found the place between her thighs. Jessica glared at him, but she was unable to resist. She opened her legs wider to give him better access. In a few moments, she murmured to him, 'Don't move. The motion of the train will do the rest.' Her face concentrated on the release that would soon come. As she looked up at the luggage rack above, with her eyes shut, she let out a big sigh. Fortunately, the sound of her cry was covered by the noise of the brakes as the train slowed and finally stopped at the down platform of Hampstead Heath Station.

The last passenger in their compartment got off the train, and they were alone. Once the train started again, she placed her feet on the seat opposite and tried to make herself decent again. 'Wow, that was so-oo good,' she beamed in her American accent, which gave James the confidence to ask if it was now his turn.

'James, forget it,' she replied. 'This train is dirty, noisy, keeps stopping, and we never know who is getting on or off. Look, I have to change trains at Gunnersbury Station for the underground line. There is a deserted woman's room at the end of the platform where we can do what we like to each other—okay? Is that a deal?' she asked.

James gulped. He had never had a relationship like this before, but it sounded good. 'Well … err, yes of course I can wait,' he replied, trying to sound like a gentleman, but then he started to think about their last encounter. 'Jessica,' he asked sheepishly, 'tell me what happened last time when you got off the train … err, just before Hampstead Station. That made a bit of a fool of me.'

'My dear James,' she replied wiping the perspiration off his brow with a damp hanky, 'I didn't disappear; I just moved up a couple of compartments on my own and thought you would follow. Sorry, but I don't usually get so personal on meeting a young man for the first time. It's just one of those things … although, yes, I did regret it after. That's why I really wanted to see you again today, before I left London.'

James was starting to get suspicious of this young woman. 'Look,' he said, 'first you were telling me about your research, that we humans are somehow related to flower bulbs, and then you were making a film today with a pop star at Broad Street Station! Can you prove any of this has really happened? Jessica looked at James long and hard. She was still on a high from her recent pleasure. Finally, she held out her left arm, and an opaque screen dropped down. James looked on in amazement as Jessica went on. 'Here we are in 1984—McCartney released the film *Give my regards to Broad Street*, which was partly filmed at Broad Street Station. Read the note. It says that the film was a flop, but the sound track went on be nominated for a Golden Globe award. These guys, Lennon and McCartney, wrote good music at that time. Look at the songs they recorded—"Good Day Sunshine", "Yesterday", and "The Long and Winding Road". Sorry, James. You may not know any of these. They haven't been released yet in 1983, have they?'

'Well, actually some of these tracks have been on the radio—from their latest LP,' replied James.

'Maybe,' said Jessica, and to prove her point, she went on. 'What about the ballad 'No More Lonely Nights'—ever heard of that?' Because, if you look here ..." And the image on the screen dangling from her harm moved up through the years. 'This song will be included in the *High School Musical* film of 2005. See? Same song sung by the loving couple—Troy and Gabriella?' James was looking at her now with a certain amount of caution. He knew that some people, including his mother, could move through time, but this was different. The years dropped back on the screen to 1983 again, and he saw an entry in bright red. He looked at Jessica carefully and begged to see this event in more detail. The entry was brief, as James read on: '23 October 1983—241 U.S. marines and 56 French troops are killed in two bomb attacks on Military headquarters in Beirut, Lebanon. The suicide bombers are thought to belong to a group of Shia Muslims based in Syrian-occupied eastern Lebanon.'

James said nothing; he just stared at Jessica in disbelief. Finally, it was Jessica who broke the silence. As she spoke, the screen receded into her arm. 'You realize, James, that this will happen in only three months' time, and there is little we can do to stop it. However, we may need you to go there some time, when you have more experience. Remember what your mother told you—you can visit, see, and observe, but should not interfere with the future, right?'

James just nodded; he knew about the other side and replied, 'so you don't really do research in the United States, do you? All that mumbo jumbo about genes and studying evolution isn't really true, is it?'

'Sorry,' she said quietly. 'I was forgetting that, in your time, research on human DNA is still incomplete, but you should get there in the next decade. The results may come as a bit of a shock. The screen you saw is a genetic addition we have made to the human arm and is triggered by electrical impulses from my brain. By the way, I do still work in Albuquerque, but it's a long way off in the future.'

James looked at what he had thought was such a simple holiday girl and sighed. 'Can you tell me what it's like there now?'

She replied, 'You know I can't explain everything, but in New Mexico we're okay. It's the continental north that has suffered.'

James looked at her. Guessing, he said, 'Because of a big change in the climate?'

Jessica nodded and replied, 'It started with a volcanic eruption about five hundred years from your time. Europe is now covered with ice that's over a mile thick, and there is no one living north of the thirty-fifty parallel in the United States. Even in New Mexico, at 5,000 feet, we are right on the limit. You can guess what happened to the rest of life on the planet, living space is much reduced.'

James just sat there looking at her as the news sank in. Finally, it was Jessica who brought him back to Earth, or rather the train, which had now reached Willesden Junction. With only three more stops to Gunnersbury, she said, 'I need to give you some more training, if you are going to be able to help us. How much do you know about time travel? You must have moved forwards and backwards in time, James.'

'Yes, my mother taught me how to "trip out" with out-of-body experiences. It's weird at first leaving your body behind, but there are good things to see—like you can meld with the girls!' He bragged, 'Lots of people do that at night when sleeping, but I also use it to sort out things at work, if I don't trust someone or can't see an answer clearly. The main problem with time travel is that the windows in timeare continually changing locations, so you can't always go where you want. The further you go into the future, the longer the cycles get. Although I can travel one year ahead, I often can't get into a time zone two or three years ahead? Also I find that going back in time decreases my astral powers to see clearly, but when I go forward in time, my body weight increases, so maybe we can affect events in the future after all?'

'No, that's not what I mean,' she explained. 'That's astral travel. Have you ever jumped from one place to another inside your own body?' asked Jessica.

'Well, no, that's not possible is it?' James asked. 'I mean, only your astral body can pass through objects because it's so light, but a solid body would get stopped, wouldn't it?'

'Not if you know how,' was the reply. 'Okay, first let's float up to the luggage rack opposite.' Their spirit bodies sat there holding hands. 'Now I'll go up the train and look for another empty compartment. You just stay here, right.'

James suddenly had no intention of going anywhere; in fact, he was starting to feel very nervous about this new idea. He put his jacket back on and took his briefcase down from the rack, clutching it to his chest. Five seconds later, Jessica appeared at his side again, smoothing down her white skirt and looking pleased. 'There is an empty compartment two down that way. Now take my hand and prepare yourself to jump down the train into that empty compartment.' Jessica quickly disappeared, but James stayed where he was. She returned, seemingly annoyed at his lack of progress. 'Take your spirit to see the empty compartment yourself!' she commanded. He was there and back in a flash. 'Right,' she said. 'Now stand up and hold onto your briefcase.' Moving behind him, she put her arms around his body. They disappeared together and then reappeared in the empty compartment, with her arms still around him.

'Wow!' was all James said as the train, with much noise from the brakes, pulled into Gunnersbury Station, and they both sat down on the seat together, laughing.

As soon as the train came to a stop, Jessica stood up to open the door. With James behind her, they both alighted from the train. Jessica took his hand and ran down the platform towards a building at the far end of the station. They ran past the guard on the train blowing his whistle at the sight of her long bare legs, and soon the carriages moved off again. Gunnersbury Station was served by both the North London Line and underground trains. Built above ground on the north side of the Thames River, it held the headquarters of the London Transport Board and a large goods yard, now mainly derelict. The station consisted of a large, red brick Victorian house containing the original booking office, waiting room, and offices for the railway staff. Joined onto the main building was a small house containing the toilets. The entrance to the ladies' lavatory was at the far end of the building, facing two large tunnels.

Jessica opened the door and walked into what was a typical Victorian lavatory. It had a red tiled floor, two cubicles, and two porcelain washbasins, with a cracked mirror above on the wall. As soon as James saw it was empty, he entered, carefully closing the door behind him. It was, as Jessica had said, clean and smelt of a strong disinfectant. She turned to face James, slowly pulling up the hem of her skirt. 'So, James, we finally made it here. And, as promised, you can do what you like with me.' She laughed. James hardly knew what to say or do, as he had always been the one in charge before. Jessica held out her arms and tried to pull him towards her. But now it was James who resisted, as he took off his jacket and placed his briefcase on the floor under one of the washbasins.

'Look,' she almost pleaded, 'I have less than twenty minutes before my connection arrives, so you had better get started.' After a couple of minutes of kissing, James was starting to feel more confident. He turned her around and bent her over the washbasin. When she was in place, he simply pulled up her short skirt. Pulling his zipper down, he slowly entered her from behind. Jessica was ready from before, as James moving faster and faster in the hot summer evening. He brought them both to a final release and fell to his knees on the floor panting from his exertions. Finally he was able to stand and blurted out, 'Thanks! That was great. I think you really are a terrific girl.'

Jessica, already standing up, splashed cold water on her flushed face and turned to James. 'May I have my panties back?' James opened his briefcase and handed them to her. 'You know, James,' she said in a superior voice, 'you still have a lot to learn about travel to the other side.' She slipped into her panties. 'As you mentioned before, time zones are continually changing, and I have calculated that the future where I want to go will cross present time on the platform outside in about ten minutes, so I have to get moving. It's going to take a lot of energy to make this work, so I want you to stay in here until all the noise has stopped, okay?'

James just nodded, at that moment; he would have done anything she asked. Jessica gave him a quick kiss and started to move towards the door. James gave her a puzzled look and asked, 'Have you done this before?'

'No, it's the first time, I'm afraid,' she admitted. 'Your generation haven't built a high-energy particle accelerator yet, so we are going to try it with a tube tunnel and all the electricity on your underground network. That's why we had to come to this station.' She smiled at him. 'By the way, after our little liaison just now, I hope to send your daughter back in about twenty years, if this works out. All right?'

Dumbfounded, James exclaimed, 'What? And just how am I going to recognise her?'

'You won't have too; she will find you. Look, I have to go.' She turned away from him, and then turned back and laughed. 'One more thing, James. Pull up your zipper. You're in the ladies' toilet after all! Wish me luck, and thanks. You were great.' And with that, Jessica was gone.

James washed his face with cold water and glanced at the mirror. He looked a wreck; his shirt was half out of his trousers and his tie almost undone. Soon after there was a rushing sound outside, like a whirlwind. It was a sound he had never heard before. As the whirlwind penetrated the ladies' loo, he fell on his knees and clung onto the basin waste pipe as his briefcase was being sucked along the floor. He reached out and grabbed it before it flew away. Whatever was going on outside sounded most violent and must be doing structural damage to the building. Suddenly it stopped, as quickly as it had started, and James made for the door at last. When he ventured outside, he saw no one, just a lot of dust and debris still floating in the air. Slate tiles from the roof littered the platform. There was no sign of Jessica either, but he could see that the rails going into one of the tunnels were buckled. Hearing voices approaching down the platform, he turned and walked around the other side of the building and found himself outside the men's toilet. Needing time to think of a plan of escape, he ventured in, but when he looked in the mirror, he saw that his face was sunburnt and bright red. When he opened his shirt, he saw his chest was burnt as well. Even the skin on his legs was burnt. Whatever had passed into that tunnel had gone with some force and must have x-rayed the front of his body. He frantically searched in his pocket for some sun cream, but there was none. Then he remembered he had an old stamp pad in his brief case. He pulled out a small tin of blue dye and smeared this on his hands, face and neck. The dye turned the redness into a dark brown colour. He thought this might just pass as a dark suntan.

Straightening his tie and smoothing his hair, he went out onto the platform again, only to walk straight into one of the railway foremen, a West Indian with almost the same colour skin. 'Hey, man, are you the guy who was with that blonde in a short skirt?' he questioned James.

'No idea what you are talking about,' James lied. 'I just came out the men's toilet, and I'm looking for the next train home to Richmond,' he retorted.

'Well you're going to have to take the bus,' replied the foreman. 'All the lines have been bent by something real strange. Are you sure you didn't see this girl?' James just shook his head and walked off towards the station exit. Then, on hearing police sirens approaching, he headed up a nearby flight of stairs towards the road outside. When he got to the top of the stairs, he found the stairwell had been closed off with a wire fence, which was almost eight feet high and impossible to climb. A moment later, he could see police officers running down the station entrance towards the platforms, and a railway worker was pointing at James, who was now trapped at the top of the stairs. Outside was Chiswick High Road leading down to Kew Bridge and his home in Richmond. There was already a small queue of commuters waiting for a London bus home. James thought he might pass his astral body through the wire, but that would leave his physical body still on the inside and only raise more questions from the police.

Just as he thought there was no way to escape, he noticed a London tramp sitting on the pavement in the shade. He looked again and saw that the man was wearing an old overcoat. He knew he had seen it before. Suddenly he realized that it was his guardian sitting there, and he shouted out at him. The man slowly turned, rose to his feet, and approached James smiling. 'Hello, James. Got yourself into a spot of trouble there, I see.'

James was relieved to see him. 'I've got to get over the fence!' he said.

'Sorry, that's not possible,' said the guardian. 'But, if you place your face, torso, arms, legs, and feet against the wire, I'll pull you through. It should be quite easy.'

James did as he was asked, and his guardian's hands passed straight through the wire and seized James's wrists. At that point, the wire around his body and legs became opaque, and James fell forward onto the pavement. As soon as he was through, his guardian withdrew his hands, and the wire returned to its former solid state. James was too stunned to notice any of this. A small crowd of passers-by gathered around to see James on his knees, with his jacket torn in two places. Then the crowd saw the damage to the station roof. They also saw the police down on the railway tracks. The crowd moved forward against the wire fence to see what was happening there. 'Quick, James,' said his guardian, 'now's your chance to slip away.' And with that, he also disappeared into the crowd. James got to his feet, still holding his briefcase. Apologizing to no one in particular, he said,

'Excuse me, must have tripped over ...' And he headed off straight for the queue at the bus stop. No one noticed him go.

James boarded the first bus to Richmond, paid his fare on the platform, and went upstairs to the upper deck. Although it was crowded, he was able to find a seat by the window. He sat down and surveyed the damage to his summer clothes. The arms of his suit were torn in two places, so he carefully took the jacket off, folded it up neatly, and placed it in his empty briefcase. He then noticed his trousers were also torn, and blood had trickled down his leg. He found his handkerchief in his trouser pocket and tied it around the cut on his leg. If these people really were from the future, why couldn't they do their teleporting tricks without half killing him? After a bit, he calmed down as the bus continued down Kew Road, past the famous Kew Gardens on the right. It was still very warm and light for a July evening, and the last visitors were leaving the gardens, pushing wheel chairs and prams and taking their young children home. James started to dream about Jessica and wondered if she had made it home as well.

Shortly after the bus arrived in the centre of Richmond, he descended the stairs and got off right opposite a telephone kiosk. He suddenly thought he had better call his wife and tell her he would be late coming home. He found a ten pence coin in his pocket and called his flat. She was not surprised that he was late and said that there had been an electricity failure on the underground and many commuters had had to walk home—or so the TV reporters had said. He told her he was going to relax at his fitness club for an hour or so, but secretly thought that Jessica had done one hell of a job.

James walked up a narrow street to the Richmond Health and Fitness Club, which was a modern replica of an imposing Georgian house. On opening the heavy entrance door, he was greeted by the receptionist. 'Wow, James, that's quite a tan you've got there. Been away on holidays?'

'Yes, we went to the Bahamas,' replied James with the first thing that came to his mind.

'Do you need a squash court tonight or are you just here to relax?' enquired the girl.

'No, I really need a shower after the journey home. I had a terrible time commuting tonight. All the tube trains were cancelled … again!' And he walked off downstairs to the men's locker room.

He opened his locker and carefully hung his damaged suit up on a hanger. He would have to ditch that later. Stripping off the rest of his clothes and taking a towel, he made his way to the showers. The front of his body was red all over, including his feet, and he wondered if this "particle accelerator" was also radioactive. He showered for over twenty minutes, washing his hair three times, just in case. Fortunately there was no one else around. Using his towel to cover his body, he went back to his locker. He put on a blue cotton tracksuit and made his way to the spa centre to see if any of the masseurs was still there. A big bouncy Dutch girl called Yvette was at the desk and laughed out loud when she saw his face. 'James, what have you been up to today? Fall asleep in the park?'

James just replied, 'Look, this is pretty painful. Can you do anything to help?' She ushered him into one of the massage rooms and told him to strip off his clothes while she got some calamine lotion and skin creams. 'You know, James, you really should go to a hospital with skin burns like this. It looks as if you were on one of those sun beds. Really, I don't know what you boys do in the city these days.' Taking a big piece of cotton wool, she gently applied the lotion all over James's arms, body, and legs. 'And you're not going to get much action out of that pink thing between your legs this weekend either!' James was so embarrassed he said nothing. 'Now, let that dry for about ten minutes, and we'll apply some colour, or your wife is going to be very suspicious, isn't she, James?' When she had finished, James felt better. When he looked into the mirror his face looked just well-tanned.

'Thanks, Yvette that looks great. Now I really do owe you one,' he said.

The girl replied, 'Well, you could take me out for dinner—when your suntan's better, of course.' And they were back to flirting with each other again. James said good night and, giving her a kiss, went up upstairs to the health club bar and ordered a pint of the best bitter. The ten o'clock news was just starting on the TV, and the international headline on the ITN channel was about more unrest and violence in Beirut, Lebanon. James thought about what Jessica had told him and watched a clip of gunfire on the streets in the east of the city. Next came the home news about a failure of electricity on the London underground caused by what could only be described as a 'twister' in west London. Fortunately, this had hit a deserted railway yard in Gunnersbury, so there were no reported deaths or injuries. James was pleased at this report, as it meant that Jessica must have left as she planned. The announcer switched to a man from the MET office who gave a meteorological explanation of the incident. This 'natural phenomenon' had resulted from the continuing high temperatures over London coupled with something unusual about the displacement of the jet stream south of the UK.

James was surprised how any news channel was able to get such a cover-up story in just three hours. But, if it was now being reported as a natural phenomenon, and no one was injured, there was little risk the police would be looking for witnesses. He opened his briefcase to check that his contract to work at the bank in Geneva was still there and thought it was definitely time to leave old London town, before he got into any more trouble.

Chapter 3—Sunny Climes

Antigua, West Indies—Monday, 23 January 1995

Inexhaustibly, being at one time what was to be said and at another time what has been said, the saying of you remains the living of you, never to be said ...
—Martin Carter,Caribbean verse

James was walking along the Dickenson Bay enjoying its white sand and gently lapping waves after the long flight from London Heathrow Airport in England. He had been here before in 1988 when things had been so difficult, and he had feared for his life. Coming back after seven years was not going to be easy, but he had just got divorced and needed a break ... some time alone for a change.

He tried to remember when he received the first letter at the bank in Geneva. It had come from a most unusual person, and had been addressed to the manager. The words had been quite simple: *'Dear Sir, I hope you are well and are enjoying your life in Switzerland. We all remember this time of the year, when the snow finally melts and the flowers show their colour in the hedgerows, and we enjoy the sounds of babbling streams and happy children.'* What came next was much more of a shock: *'We can only meet our families on a lawn dotted with picnic tables, shielded from the bright sun by big beach umbrellas. In the circumstances, there will be problem to pay interest on your promissory notes, for some time to come ...'*

James had taken the letter upstairs to the director of the bank, who, on seeing the letter, had said, 'Well, it looks from the postmark as if this client is in a U.S. federal prison camp somewhere near Atlanta, and our problems may have just started.' A lot of water had flowedunder the bridge since then. The bank in Antigua, together with the government, had dug itself into a hole with the United States that it would never climb out of. James had left this nightmare situation in 1988 to join a friendlier bank in Geneva, where he had adapted to the new and growing business of private banking.

Thinking little of the past, he had moved on to help solve some credit problems with the Italian government, which, after years of pressure, had at last been resolved. Shortly after that, his manager had asked if he would like to assist with a small problem in Antigua. 'Just a short assignment, nothing to do with our bank, you understand, more a question of international security, will you do it?' he asked and handed him a telephone number in London. James had read in the press that things had gone very badly wrong on the island, after he had left and was intrigued to know what had happened now. After a number of calls to the person in London, he was told to go to the international departure desk at London Heathrow to collect his ticket, which included a two-week reservation at the luxury Sandy Cove Hotel. Someone was being very generous with him, and at the time he had been delighted; now he was not so sure.

James had read in the press that non co-operation by the government of Antigua had started the previous year when Antigua simply stopped answering U.S. communications. Despite considerable diplomatic pressure, no one knew the background or the local players better than James. He had arrived with just one rendezvous on his agenda: to have dinner on the hotel terrace that evening, during which he would be briefed.

He paddled a bit in the water on the beach and then took the short walk back to the hotel to change for dinner. Putting on a more formal short-sleeve shirt and cotton slacks, he walked from his veranda room on the first floor down to the hotel lobby. The air was still hot and humid and was full of perfume as the tall palm trees swayed in the evening breeze.

Walking across to reception, he checked to see if there were any messages for his room and turned to see who might be waiting in the lobby. In the middle of January, it was just the usual crowd of retired American tourists enjoying a welcome drink on arrival at the hotel. James turned left and went towards the terrace restaurant where he was expected. He took a small table in the corner by the beach and ordered a cold beer. The minutes ticked away, and a waitress asked if he was eating alone or expecting a guest. As he was about to answer, he noticed a familiar face approach his table. James almost dropped his beer with surprise; it was Virginia Martinat, someone he knew very well; in fact, she had helped him over seven years ago. 'Hello, James, long time no see?'

He rose to his feet and embraced her and kissed her on the cheek. 'Well,' he replied,

'I didn't expect to see you again, b—but I'm delighted!' To his dismay, he found himself stammering. She was wearing a long, brown Indian print dress that showed off her figure in the evening light. Her brown hair was still long and a bit wild, which made her more interesting.

'Sorry I'm a bit late,' she went on without any explanation. 'So, James, what do you think of the hotel now? I arranged your room here as I know you liked it last time. And tell me, what have you been up to in Geneva?'

James waved his arm at the waitress and asked Virginia what she would like to drink. She ordered a glass of chilled white wine, and James started to update his old contact, using her old familiar nickname. 'Well, Gina, after I left here in '88, I moved on to another bank, which seemed like the best thing to do at the time. Made a new start in commercial banking, got divorced, and have spent the last three years in a dispute with the Italian government.' 'You got divorced?' she exclaimed with eyes raised and a lips forming a smile. 'Well I did the same after my husband left. But I've stayed on here as a single. It hasn't been easy for any of us, has it James?'

James noticed that her bare foot was rubbing against his ankle, but she just smiled at him again. James thought it was time to take the initiative and decided to ask her what his visit was all about. 'Look, I've read the press reports,' he said. 'The bank here was caught laundering a few million dollars. There were reports about arms smuggling up at the fruit farm, which all sounds pretty lame to me. Now you know as well as I do that this man will simply hire the best U.S. lawyers and run circles around the U.S. administration for a year or two. Then I would expect the U.S. authorities to start a civil law suit, just like we will do in the Italian courts, and bring the whole thing to a close in a couple of years' time. Really, it's the end game. He's already got the full attention of the FBI, the CIA, the DEA, and probably all the other agencies in Washington, so why do you need me here as well?'

'Wow, James, you don't change do you? Always straight to the point. Shall we order?' James looked at her again and had a sudden impulse to get up and kiss her. He was also sure that, in the tropical air, she would not be wearing much underwear. They ordered and spent the next hour reminiscing about the past. He realized it was better that they made small talk about what little fun they'd had in the past, as other guests had now arrived on the terrace for dinner. Gina was starting to attract glances from several older men. They had finished off a bottle of rosé wine and sat looking at each other as coffee was served. It was Gina who restarted the conversation. 'So you see, James, we look like a honeymoon couple here.' James blinked. 'Why don't I come up to your room in about fifteen minutes … say around ten? And we can discuss the details.' With that she got up and headed for the ladies' toilet, leaving James to sign the check. As he walked past the bar, he asked the barman for a chilled bottle of champagne, a bucket, and some ice. Placing a white serviette over his little surprise, he whistled to himself as he went outside again, back to his room off the first floorveranda.

Placing the champagne next to the bed, he sat down for a moment and thought, *How did she know I was coming? And who is she working for anyway?* He turned down all the lights except one by the bed, brushed his teeth in anticipation, and waited. Just after ten, there was a knock on his door, and she came straight inside. James took her into his arms and kissed her fully on the lips. His arms pulled her close to his body, and his hands ran up and down her cotton dress. To his surprise, she pulled away from him and whispered, 'James, not now. We have other things to do.' Placing her fingers against his lips, she made it clear that someone was listening to all they said. 'Oh! James,' she said brightly, 'and you brought up champagne! Let's put on a film to get us really in the mood. Before he could say anything, she turned on the TV, selected a pay channel with a good film, and left it running at full volume. Next she picked up the bottle of champagne and, taking James by the hand, pulled him outside his room, onto the veranda. 'There that should keep the goons busy for the next ninety minutes! Come on, we've got work to do!' Before James locked his door, he looked back and could see a couple already hard at it on his TV.

Gina shouted at him in low whisper, 'Come on, James!' And, taking his hand, she led him off down the stairs and away from the hotel. Once outside in the dark, James pushed her up against one of the huge palm trees. 'What the hell is going on?' he demanded.

'We're going to take a taxi to the airport to check on an arrival,' Gina explained. James kissed her again and placed his knee firmly between her legs. She gave no resistance at all. 'Look, why not take your car?' he suggested. 'You must have brought it here.'

'No, James, it's not as simple as that. Everyone visiting the hotel is checked in and out by security. I had to park my car at the restaurant next door and walk around by the beach so I wouldn't be seen. That's why I was a bit late. Now come on, or we're going to be late for our visitor.' James started to realize she must have done this before—he was once again in at the deep end.

As they approached the taxis waiting in line outside the hotel, Gina went into overdrive. Making it clear she was a drunk with a bottle in her hand, she placed her arm around James and pulled him against her as they almost fell against the back door of the first taxi. James helped her inside. 'Well, I must say your amateur dramatics have improved since we were last together,' whispered James with a chuckle.

Gina quickly replied, 'Kiss me, James, and put your hand on my knee.' James obeyed as the security guard shone a flashlight into the taxi, so could see what was going on inside. 'Sorry folks,' was all he said, and let the car proceed along the road and out of the hotel property. James looked up to see the West Indian driver with a big smile on his face. Gina sat up and smoothed down her dress again, opened her window, and threw the bottle out into the bamboo hedgerow.

'Sorry James, if we drink that, you won't be of any use to me at all tonight!'

V.C. Bird International Airport, Antigua

As the taxi approached the airport terminal, the driver turned to them. 'international arrivals?' he asked. But Gina asked him to drive past the armed guard patrolling the entrance, to a small door at the far end of the building. When they arrived, James paid the fare and followed Gina to the door marked 'Security Staff Only'. She inserted a plastic card into a security terminal next to the door, the door buzzed open, and they went inside the airport. They descended down some concrete steps to a low wall, just before the tarmac, with a clear view of the runway. There was a large American-style ambulance parked in front of them, and a white orderly jumped out and came across to talk to them. 'Evening, Miss Martinat. You just made it in time. The plane from Miami should be arriving any minute.'

'Thanks,' was all Gina replied.

'Now don't you two get any ideas of coming out onto the runway,' warned the orderly. 'They have just installed security cameras all over this area, and we don't want to raise more suspicions, do we?' The man got into the ambulance and drove it off to a holding position just before the runway. Gina fell back into James arms against the wall. He placed his hands over her tummy and pulled her against him. As their faces fixed on the small plane that was just coming in for al landing, James was puzzled. 'Gina, I've seen this before,' he said. 'But usually it's visitors to the island who suffer a heart attack and get flown *out* on an ambulance plane. It's usually not the other way around.'

Gina looked at him and replied, 'Well, James, the difference this time is that the man arriving tonight is already dead.'

The small private jet came to a stop just in front of the ambulance, and a number of uniformed officials came out of the airport terminal onto the tarmac. James sighed at the delay and started to nibble at Gina's right ear lobe. Her hair smelt of frangipani perfume, and he was getting turned on. 'Stop it, James. You know that excites me.' He felt her body go rigid. 'Look, here they come now. Just follow me.' The ambulance returned in a big circle and parked near them with its doors facing the terminal, so it was difficult to see what happened inside. The driver came down and opened the wide doors at the back. James saw it was empty except for a black body bag. It was Gina who then jumped up into the back of the ambulance and, giving James her hand, pulled him up inside. The orderly switched on the inside light then quickly got out and closed the doors behind them.

Gina pulled down the zip fastening on the body bag. 'Steady, James,' she warned him. 'This is not going to be pleasant.' James looked at the body. It was dressed in a khaki uniform and appeared to be bloated from immersion in seawater. What James noticed immediately was that his skin all over his face was burnt. As Gina opened the man's shirt, he realized that the burns extended over his chest. James looked quickly to check that the man's bare feet were the same colour. By now, the smell started to overpower both of them. Gina quickly zipped the body bag up again, and they both clung onto each other for a moment. James thought he was going to be sick and hammered on the doors to be let out. When the doors opened, they both fell on the ground, gasping at the clean fresh air. 'Well, I did warn you,' said the driver to them both. He turned and got back into the ambulance, this time in the driver's seat. Pulling up her long dress, Gina climbed into the cab and sat in the middle of the bench seat. James followed her. The orderly drove the ambulance out of the cargo exit, and soon they were travelling away from the airport, driving west, down Burma Road.

Cassada Gardens, Antigua

As they reached the countryside, Gina turned to the driver and asked if he would drop them both off at her house in Cassada Gardens. The driver just nodded as if he had expected that, but said nothing. After about ten minutes, he drew up outside a small bungalow. It was surrounded by a low fence; a wooden gate opened onto a garden path. It looked like a typical small, English house, and James found himself thinking it could be anywhere in Devon. They both got out of the ambulance. Gina thanked the driver for his help, and with that, the ambulance disappeared into the night. 'I remember this house from last time,' said James, but Gina just took his arm and hurried him up to the front door. Looking under a stone, she found the spare key and opened the door.

Once inside, James took her face in his hands, and they dove into a long and much-needed kiss. Her hands fumbled with the belt on his trousers, but James was having none of that. He roughly pulled her dress up over her shoulders, until, with her arms in the air, she was naked before him. He lifted her up into his arms and carried her through into the bedroom. He gently placed her on the four-poster bed. She watched him in anticipation as he took off his clothes before joining her.

By the time they had finished, they were both covered in sweat. James looked down at a bead of perspiration running down between her breasts and grinned. 'Well, James, was it really worth coming back again to this island?'

James replied, 'No, not really.' He placed his finger in her mouth, and she bit him hard with her front teeth. 'God!' he said. 'What was that for?' But they both knew and laughed. Finally, Gina got up and turned on the air conditioning in the room. Then she carefully lowered the mosquito nets around the bed. By the time she came back, it was a bedroom scene from the past. Gina lowered her naked body onto James and started to rub his nose, until James was about to sneeze. Finally he broke the spell. 'Who was the man in the ambulance?' he asked.

'James, that's not important, but you saw something you have seen before, didn't you? Have you seen people exposed to such levels of radiation in the past?'

James just nodded and scratched his head. 'Well, it once happened to me, more than ten years ago,' he finally said.

Gina got off the bed and went out of the room. When she came back, she had a bottle of scotch and two glasses. She lay on her side next to him and entwined her legs with his while James poured a generous measure into each glass. 'Cheers,' she said. 'It's not another of your girlfriend stories is it?'

James looked at the amber liquid in his glass and grinned. 'Really, I have no idea how to explain it to you. I met this American girl on a commuter train in north London, got talking and you know … well, she seduced me in the ladies' lavatory on a tube station!' he stammered.

'James, not exactly up to your usual high standard of female care, is it?'

'No, but this was different. Look, Gina, first of all this person was from a different time from ours! She showed me things that would happen months ahead, and they happened. We went on astral travels together on the train, and she knew how the time zones are always changing. Then, after we had sex, she just went outside onto the platform and disappeared.'

'Okay, James. Let's say I believe all that. But what's it got to do with high-level radiation burns?'

'Sorry, yes there is a lot more to the story. Just before she left, she said something about needing a high-energy particle accelerator. Then, when she went into the tube station, there was one almighty noise, which destroyed half the station roof, and I was left with radiation burns on the entire front of my body. They didn't heal for weeks to! The BBC reported it as a twister over west London—a complete cover-up story, if you ask me.'

'Thank you, James. You have just confirmed what you are doing here in my bed,' Gina replied with some satisfaction on her face at last. 'I read about that incident; didn't it take out all the electrical power from the underground at the same time?'

'Yes,' replied James. 'So you believe me—and the time travel story? Can it really be made to happen?'

'Well, that's what you are doing here on Antigua,' said Gina. 'I do know all about astral travel. My mother taught me how to do it in France when I was little. In fact, that is how I found you and realized you could help us here.'

'Really? Will you do it with me now?' said James looking excited.

'Well, I've never been with a man before in the astral world, and I guess you've had lots of girls, haven't you, James?'

'Yes, but it's different. It's not sexual like tonight, but a warm feeling of comfort and security. Now let's fill up our glasses and say bottoms up to this new experience together!' James poured a generous portion into each glass, and they drank it down in one shot. James needed a bit of attention, so Gina went down on him, and when, he was ready, he stretched his legs out on the bed and leaned back. Gina mounted him with no difficulty and sat down on his thighs. They wrapped their arms around each other and kissed as their astral bodies floated up above the canopy. James finally thought he had reached his heaven, as they both drifted off into an astral sleep together.

Hours later, he awoke to the smell of bacon and eggs cooking in the kitchen. On looking up, he could see Gina standing at the stove in a white T-shirt and little else. Minutes later, she approached the bed with a tray laden with a plate of English breakfast and two glasses of orange juice. 'Good morning, sir,' she said in a cheeky voice. 'You have slept well; it's past ten in the morning, and were up to no good last night, eh!' James knew from experience that, whatever you did with a woman in the night, she made you pay for it the next morning. He gave her a kiss and let his hand slowly trail up her naked thigh. 'No,' she warned him. 'No more of that. We've got work to do today. First you have to go back to your hotel and get my car. The keys are in the exhaust pipe, right. Then in the afternoon, at three thirty, we have a meeting out at the U.S. base to discuss the body you saw last night,' she explained. 'I've also got a file for you to read at the hotel, but bring it back please.'

As James's head started to clear, he asked if the base was close to the squash court they had played on last time they'd seen each other. 'Well, yes,' replied Gina. 'Why do you ask?'

'And what time is our meeting?' asked James.

'Scheduled for three thirty this afternoon'

'Well, then,' said James, 'we can have a game of squash at two and go on to the meeting afterwards. Really, I can't wait to chase you all over the squash court again!' With that, James leapt out of bed and went to shower.

Gina cleared the breakfast plates into the kitchen while James was getting dressed and then called a taxi, so James was ready to leave the house in less than thirty minutes. 'All right, darling,' he said, 'I should be back here at one thirty to pick you up. I'll have your car and a squash racquet!' Then he thought and went on, 'Could you rent me a car from Leeward Motors for a week and have it delivered here by the time I get back? Just a small salon car ... nothing flashy, you know.' And with that he was gone.

Men, she thought. *Most of the time they are quite impossible.* But their melding together last night had given her an insight into his past experience, and she could see it was frightening.

Old Navy Base, Antigua—Tuesday, 24 January 1995

James was back at the hotel in less than twenty minutes and went straight up to his room. The TV had been turned off, but nothing else looked disturbed. The French windows onto his balcony were open, and he could see that tourists were already sitting on the beach in the morning sun. He kicked off his shoes and collapsed on his bed to read the file Gina had given him. Most of it referred to the arms smuggling activities up at the fruit farm, where the land had been taken over by the bank to develop into a holiday resort. *Nothing very new about that,* he thought just as there was a knock on his door. He got up and opened the door and was confronted by an attractive young woman in a smart hotel uniform. She had dark black hair and a deep suntan. *Middle East origin*, he thought as she introduced herself. 'Hello.' She smiled. 'My name's Shoshanna, your entertainment hostess. You must be James, err ...' She looked at her hotel clipboard. 'James Pollack, right?' James nodded. She shook James's hand and went on. 'We just wanted to be sure that you have settled in, and we'd like to invite you to a barbeque we're having at eight tonight. It's your first time on the island is it?' James ignored her last question and advised he was fine. For some unknown reason he also told her that he had hired a car to explore more of the island. Before he knew it, she had pushed her way into his room to point out the new bathroom fittings they had recently installed. *Damn this woman*, thought James as he realized that she must have seen the file lying open on his bed. He quickly flipped it shut and assured her he would be delighted to come to the barbeque. 'See you at eight,' he assured her. 'Wouldn't miss it for the world.' And he ushered her out of his room.

After she left, James changed into his brief swimsuit, a pair of khaki shorts, white tennis shirt, and some old squash shoes he had brought with him. Then, wrapping Gina's file in a beach towel, he made his way down to the hotel beach bar and ordered a cold beer and some chips. Feeling more refreshed, he watched as couples came in from the heat to rest out of the midday sun. James waited until it looked quiet. Then, leaving the bar, he walked down to the sea and sallied along the beach, towards the resort next door. Mingling with some children there, he followed them up to the restaurant and then headed for the car park to find Gina's car. He quickly recognized the make. He walked up behind the car and, stooping to tie up his shoe, found the keys in the exhaust pipe. He got into the car and started it up.

The engine started with the air conditioning fan on at full blast, so he waited until the inside had cooled down. James drove out of the car park and then back towards Cassandra to meet up with Gina again. She was waiting for him at the gate wearing a navy blue tennis dress with a flared skirt, and carrying two squash racquets. James got out of the car and returned her car keys, as she knew the way better than he did. 'James,' she said, 'you're late, What have you been doing?'

James explained he had been questioned in his room by a hostess with a dark complexion.

'Ah,' said Gina, 'the hotel bitch!'

Nothing like a bit of competition between the girls, James thought, *to make one feel appreciated!* But he did not say anything.

'You do have the file I gave you,' Gina said.

'Yes, but I think the woman saw it on my bed,' was his reply.

'What was she doing in your room?' asked Gina.

'Looking for you, I think,' said James now on the defensive.

'Okay,' admitted Gina. 'Probably no harm done, but you have to be more careful in future.' She looked at him, obviously expecting a kiss. James obliged, but on looking carefully at her outfit, he saw that she was wearing underwear.

'Knickers?' he said. 'Surely they're not allowed when playing squash?'

'Really, James, be reasonable. After last night, you're still coming on to me ... and we have a serious meeting after our game.' They got into the car, and Gina started the engine. As they drove away, she pointed out the hire car hidden in the driveway in front of the garage. Then she drove off to the north of the island.

The squash court was a standalone brick building with an elevated tin roof built under swaying palm trees. As they approached, Gina looked inside the court and, seeing it was full of old leaves, went off to find a gardener. James went to see if there was anyone in the office to book the court in advance. The squash court was just outside the U.S. military base, which was clearly visible with its white dome, which housed the advanced monitoring equipment. James thought it must have been built for the British navy and was currently little used now that the property had been transferred to the Americans. An old timer was at the office to take his ten Antiguan dollars and said no one had played on the court for months. 'Those yanks up there,' he advised, pointing to the base, 'are too busy listening in on what's going on in the air waves.' James took his receipt and went back to find Gina. By the time he got back to the court, Gina was already warming up the ball by smashing it against the front wall. 'Come on, James,' she said. 'Your racket's in the corner. What are you waiting for?' James couldn't help but admire her long, sun-tanned legs and her short skirt, which showed off her white panties every time she hit the ball. This was going to be a replay of the game they'd had in 1988, and James had no intention of giving away any points. After only fifteen minutes, they were both covered in perspiration, and James picked up the beach towel he had brought and offered it to Gina to wipe her glowing face.

'Thanks, James, that was great,' she said. 'I've got some water in a bottle over there.' She pointed to her bag, which she'd left near the door. 'If you can get it?'

'Okay, but don't think you've finished,' warned James. 'I've yet to chase you around the court!'

Gina knew exactly what to expect from her man and just played along. First she ran to the front corner and let James kiss her briefly, and then she ran over the back of the court, where James pinned her against the wall. At this point, someone hammered on the door, and it burst open. The old man from the booking office stared at them both. 'Excuse me, miss, but the folks over there just called.' He pointed to the base. 'They say they're ready for you now.' Both of them just fell into laughter at how ridiculous the whole scene must have looked. Taking their racquets and Gina's bag, they left the court.

When they returned to the car, Gina turned the air conditioner on, and they both tried to recover from their exertions. She took the towel and wiped between her legs, then applied plenty of perfume to her body and face. 'Now, James, this is a strictly-off-the-record meeting, so no names or ID, is that clearly understood? When we get to the gate, just leave it to me to show some ID. If they insist on anything from you, just show them any old credit card, okay?' When they got to the entrance gate, a military guard came out and looked into the car. Gina flashed her ID, and James gave the guard a plastic ski pass he still had in his wallet from Christmas. The guard scratched his head took the pass inside. When he came back, he raised the barrier to let them in. A military jeep then appeared and escorted them to a parking place by the main entrance. Two armed soldiers escorted them inside to a lift where another guard was waiting for them. The lift descended into the depths of the base, and when the doors opened, there was a small welcome party waiting for them.

The first to greet them was the camp commander, a short, grey-haired professional officer who had been on the island for some years. 'Miss Martinat, welcome and delighted to see you again.' They shook hands, and he kissed her briefly once on the cheek. 'This must be your colleague from Switzerland,' he said turning to James and extending his hand. 'Good to meet you too.' Then he turned to the men accompanying him. 'Now then, let's sit down, and I'll introduce you to my colleagues. No real names, you understand, as this is ... well, not a military meeting, but to help us understand what we may be dealing with here.' James shook hands with a two-star U.S. general, responsible for surveillance, and then a wiry man who said he was a scientist from Washington. They all moved over to a conference table and sat down with Gina next to James who sat in the middle, clearly as the guest of honour. The base commander started the discussion by introducing each of the participants. When it came to James, it was intimated that he was working at an international research centre just outside Geneva and little more. James was getting more and more nervous, as he was not up to any real scientific questioning. Yes, he had once visited that centre on a guided tour, but knew little more than what he'd been told at the time. He felt Gina's hand squeeze his knee under the table, as she leaned forward and whispered in his ear, 'Relax and listen.'

The initial discussion was about how the base monitored all conversations to and from the island and all the other islands to the west, including Puerto Rico and all the way up to the Bahamas. James was surprised that they covered such a big area. Then the base commander explained the reason behind this meeting. About six months ago, a U.S. naval patrol vessel had found a body in the sea about 120 miles north of Antigua, wearing a life jacket packed with drugs. 'Nothing very surprising about that in this area,' he said. Then another body was found by a U.S. Coast Guard ship some fifty miles from U.S. waters, and they started to take an interest. Over the next three months, more bodies were found in the sea, and all of them had suffered from the same high-radiation burns all over their bodies, and most found in a northerly direction. At that same time, NASA scientists in Florida were inspecting this equipment, and they had been monitoring other objects they'd tracked falling back to Earth. The general then explained that, as soon as the army got involved, they had brought the latest equipment down to the base on Antigua to see if they could track down the source and origin of these objects. 'The objects are acquired at a height of about 3,000 feet,' explained the general, 'all on a northerly trajectory as if they are trying to enter U.S. air space. It's how they materialize in the atmosphere that we really don't understand. Furthermore, although they started getting closer to the Florida coast, recent monitoring shows they have now fallen back towards the island here.' He was addressing everyone around the table, but when he stopped talking, he looked directly at James. James was desperately thinking of what his children had taught him last summer, while sailing on Lake Geneva, with an experiment called Schrödinger's cat.

The American scientist just smiled at James, and James began to explain. 'A cat is placed in a sealed box that contains a mechanism that offers a fifty percent probability of an incidence of radioactive decay. When the box is opened, will the cat be dead or alive?' asked James. He put up his hand to indicate he did not expect an answer. 'The whole point of quantum mechanics,' he went on, 'is that it has a different view of reality. In the case of the cat, there are two possible outcomes—in one reality, the cat is dead, while in the other it remains alive. In quantum theory, both possibilities can exist together, so an object can exist in two places at the same time.'

Gina put her head in her handsthinking that James had blown their cover, but the scientist looked at James. "Have you worked with Stephen Hawking?' he asked.

'Not directly,' replied James, but we have studied his latest essays about black holes and baby universes, published in 1993.' Everyone around the table started to take more time to listen to James, and it was the general who now asked, 'So let's say … well, if you were to predict what would be the next development at this place of yours in Switzerland, what would be the next big project?'

James thought hard for a moment and replied, 'A high-energy particle accelerator is needed to prove these theories, but it looks as if you have one here already.' The meeting room went so quiet that James could almost hear his heartbeat. It was the base commander who replied at last, 'Thank you, James, that's what we thought as well. Gentleman, we have a lot to consider, but I think we can adjourn this meeting.'

James turned to the general. 'Can you pinpoint the source of the radiation on the island?'

The general nodded, but the commanded replied, 'As our man on the ground, you should know that it appears to be generated on the far side of Green Castle Hill, but that's all we can say.'

As the meeting broke up, hands were shaken all around, and the commander came over to talk to James alone, 'Well done, although I've no idea what that cat story of yours was all about.' Then he added, 'You pulled that off rather well, and I know you have excellent cover, but be careful … these people have good connections both in Washington and in Israel. We understand there is a new shipment coming in tonight, down in St John's. Might be worth having a look, eh!'

After saying good-bye, Gina and James were escorted back to her car. As they drove out of the base, Gina exploded. 'James, you have no right to give away confidential secrets to our American friends! Really, I can't believe it!'

James looked at her and laughed. 'Gina, I was given that information by the afternoon tour guide last summer at CERN with my boys, so really it's no big secret, although I'm sure they will check the story with London, won't they?'

'Yes,' she said, 'and that's not the only thing they are going to check on! I have to report back to London as soon as I can. Can I drop you off at the house and you can take the hire car back to the hotel?'

'Fine by me,' replied James seeing she was going to be busy for the rest of the evening.

When they arrived at his hotel, Gina stopped the car to let him out and warned, 'James, be careful with that hostess girl. I think she could be watching you.'

'No problem,' he assured her. 'I'm sure you are right. Why don't you come and have coffee with me at the hotel around ten tomorrow morning?'

'Love to,' replied Gina. And, giving him a kiss, she drove away.

St. John's Harbour, Antigua—Tuesday 24 January 1995
By the time James got back to the hotel, it was past six, and he could see the sun was going down in the west. The security guard at the gate remarked that James had been away for a few days, and James said he had been visiting one of the other islands. The guard told James to park in the visitors' parking on the right, so he knew he had been logged in.

Suddenly, James realized what he had said, and reached into the glove compartment for a map of the region. He raced down to reception to recover his key and went straight up to his room. Placing the map on a table, he drew a line from Green Hill on Antigua to the south of Montserrat and realized it went straight into a sleeping volcano. The potential was obvious—that it might erupt, which would create an environment of strong particle bombardment. James then remembered the invitation to the hotel barbeque and took of his clothes to shower.

In his robe, James went out onto his balcony. The scene was one of a tropical beach and the sun setting over the island of Montserrat, which was covered in cloud. James went back inside and dressed in his smart casual clothes and, after watching the local news on his TV, he made his way down to the hotel reception. The party had already started at the bar. There were some of the American tourists in attendance, but no one was on duty at the hostess desk. James ordered a bottle of beer and went down to the beach where a fire had been lit for the evening party. He raised his bottle to a couple of well-oiled Americans, whom, he realized, were busy chatting up Shoshanna. She was dressed in hot shorts and a coloured T-shirt. After a while, she came over to talk to him. 'Hello, James, you really are a shy one. Where have you been today, sightseeing?' she asked.

'Yes, I went down to that Nelson's Place and then onto English Harbour,' replied James, unconvincingly.

'Actually, it's Nelson's Dockyard,' she corrected him. 'And I heard you were playing squash at the other end of the island. Right? So just exactly what are you doing here?' James tried to ignore her remarks, but she continued. 'Look, James, let's be straight with each other. I've checked up, and you have a police record here, don't you? You were arrested here in January 1988 for an illegal corporate action against a close partner of the government, shortly after which you were asked to leave.'

'Well, we can't all be perfect,' replied James. 'But this time I'm here on holiday and came back to see an old friend, if you must know. Why don't I get you a drink, and we can just be friends.'

'That's all right, I can manage on my own.' And with that she went over to talk to some other guests. James had been warned by Gina. *I'm not going to put up with this from a stuck-up entertainment hostess!* he told himself. Downing his beer, he left the party before it had really even started.

James walked back through the hotel lobby, left his key at the desk, and walked up the drive to his car in the visitors' parking. He drove up Dickenson Bay Street and then down Friars Hill Road going in the direction of St. John's and started to think. As he turned down the High Street, he noticed all the new offshore banks that had set up here since last time he'd visited the island. Suddenly, he braked hard as a black cat ran across the road in front of his car. Looking up, he saw he had stopped outside the ornate offices of the Bank of Antigua, with its marble entrance, which was decorated with exotic flowers and even a small fountain. He started to wonder how all this was possible on a small tropical island, when suddenly the penny dropped. He knew that the bank in Geneva had merged with one of the oldest American names, and they had even started a joint venture together around 1989. He had heard that the bank had immediately commenced a number of joint ventures involving ships and ports in the Soviet Union, which had come to nothing. This was nothing new for this bank, which had spent years in his time trying to negotiate a Middle East pipeline deal. The many offshore companies played the part of a middleman between the U.S. administration and the Israeli government. Although it fell apart, this bank'scontacts went right to the top—the secretary of state and even the U.S. president.

Now James had another idea. What if all that had just been a long and convenient courtship, to giveprotection for a much bigger game, which would now start in the new developing Russian market? The little bank in Antigua with its small money laundering scandal was a cover, to show how easy it was to be exposed to this crime, with a corrupt British bank manager. Once he knew of the problem, he had immediately sold the bank in order to claim he was no longer responsible, but James thought that most unlikely.

In this new financial venture, the bank in Switzerland would introduce Russian banks to its American partner, who was able to offer some sort of software to their clientele banks. This permitted customers to transfer money in and out of their correspondent accounts without any real-time intervention or control by anyone, anywhere! Once these funds were in U.S. accounts, they could be moved to other offshore centres like Antigua for further distribution. That explained the sudden growth of offshore banks here. The setup was simple and attractive to both parties. The U.S. bank would make millions from these electronic money transfers, while the bank in Geneva took no responsibility for whether the transfers were legal or were hot money from the Mafia. Some transfers might even be recycled loans from the International Monetary Fund. James had read somewhere that the scale of this criminal trade ran into billions of dollars each year, transferred through the major banks, to unknown offshore companies. In addition, phony American deposit receipts (ADRs) were being sold on through U.S. brokers, to the great American investor. ADRs were issued by U.S. banks to offer a bundle of shares from foreign companies and sell them on the New York Stock Exchange. The foreign companies, often emerging Russian stocks, were meant to provide financial information to the sponsor bank, but in reality they were bankrupt from the start. James thought it would take about ten years to collapse both the U.S. and Western economies. The U.S. military may have won the cold war, but it was going to be the Red Mafia who would profit most from the economic battle for their homeland.

James parked just in front of the Heritage Quay, which he hardly recognized since his last visit. A new shopping centre had been constructed with an outdoor restaurant, which was surprisingly deserted. To his left, the old St. John's pier had been extended to take larger vessels. Against the quay was a half-lit cargo ship, discharging wooden crates onto a waiting line of trucks. James watched in amazement as next in view was a heavy low loader, which was carefully positioned beside one of the cargo holds. He knew from his time in the navy that discharging heavy loads could be tricky. As the heavy lift gantry took the weight of the cargo, the ship heeled over some ten degrees or more. James could see men in grey uniforms waving at the ship in alarm. Some of the men appeared to be carrying light arms. At that moment, there was a tap on the window of his car, and a uniformed police officer asked him what he was doing. 'This area's all been closed off tonight; didn't you see the sign back up the road?'

James apologized and was going to back up the road, when one of the security guards he has seen before approached his car. 'Okay, out, out of the car,' said the guard, waving his Galil assault rifle at

James. And, as James got out of the car, it suddenly felt quite cold, as a sea mist blew off the docks and confused both the security men for just a moment.

'Evening, James. Got yourself into a spot of trouble again, I see.' It was his guardian, whom he had not seen for over ten years. 'Now then, take my arm, and we'll both move away from here quickly—I think we have a bit of explaining to do.' James saw a bright light and heard a noise in his head, and before he knew what was happening, he found himself sitting on the road beside his car. 'Very sorry about that,' his Guardian said with a slight Indian accent. And, finally, he introduced himself. 'My name is Deepak ... Deepak Hagler. And you, of course, are James Pollack. Are you all right?'

James felt as if he had been through a mincing machine and looked down to check his arms and legs. He just nodded.

'These worm holes always make you feel a bit compressed the first time,' explained Deepak, 'but the effect should wear off quite soon.'

'Deepak, where exactly are we?' asked James. 'Have we moved? It looks like the same place we were before.'

'Well, yes it is exactly where you parked over seven years ago, when you were here on the island last time ... same place, same time of day. Well actually we're thirty minutes early, so we'll have to move on soon to make room for your other car.' James stood up and saw he was now standing beside the car he had hired years ago. The quay was undeveloped, and opposite was the new office building with an attorney's nameplate on the wall. 'Go on,' said Deepak, 'have a look through the window. You will see the fax machines receiving the legal papers you delivered up at the fruit farm last time.' James walked over to the building and peered into the offices to check Deepak's story, and then he looked at the port. There were a lot of fishing boats and no pier, no cargo ship, and no one was around from before. James shook his head in disbelief, thinking it must be a dream.

'Come on, best we get on our way,' said Deepak. James felt in his pocket for the car keys and realized he was wearing his old shorts and the same navy shirt he had worn years ago. He was starting to believe it really was 1988. 'Where are we going?' asked James as he turned the ignition key and nothing happened.

As James tried the engine again, Deepak replied, 'Up to the fruit farm, where you went last time. Can't really go anywhere else with two of you running about on the island, can we?' Finally the engine started, and James turned the car and headed out of town, up to Gray's Farm and the Valley Road. As he drove, he found he could easily remember the way. As the car struggled up the hill, James could make out a slope with a wire fence to keep visitors off the farm property. Deepak pointed to a turning off the main road, and James stopped the car under some trees. They both got out of the car and walked up the road to a gate, where a sign had been fixed: 'Strictly Private. Keep Out'. Climbing over the gate, they walked to the top of the hill where James remembered there was a good view of the farm buildings.

Deepak was sweating in the hot tropical air as James questioned him. 'Deepak, why do you wear that ridiculous winter coat every time I see you?' he asked.

'Well, I just came from Bulgaria where it's quite cold in January. Can't keep changing in my job. I have quite a number of charges to look after—well over two thousand at present. Many are getting into trouble like you. In fact, I was just helping your daughter Nathalie, who got into a scrap with her boyfriend, you see?'

'Deepak, don't be so ridiculous. If she was alive, she would be ... well, just twelve years old, wouldn't she?'

'Well, that's right, and girls grow up fast in Bulgaria. You remember how Jessica left London? Well, she flew off into the future, but poor Nathalie—or at least her DNA—stayed behind in your time. It happens sometimes with the time zone changes. So we hid her in Sofia, where no one would know. You should go and see her sometime. Really a lovely girl.It would be good for you to go to her before she comes to find you.' James was beginning to find his guardian Deepak quite interesting.

James and Deepak looked down on the farm buildings, which had been lit up with bright floodlights. The scene was much the same as he had seen before, with trucks being unloaded by a number of security guards, all armed with short submachine guns. 'Funny that a fruit farm should need such security,' remarked Deepak. 'Now watch where the trucks go to next.' James watched closely as each truck disappeared into a tunnel in the side of the hill. 'Now then, James, I'm going to explain what they are really doing down there. The tunnel down there has been excavated right under Green Castle Hill. It comes out on the west side of the Island. You can probably guess what they want to build here, but it's much more than a particle accelerator. They're testing the transformation of matter into light, which is more advanced quantum science.'

James was stunned. He replied, 'But that's already ten years ahead of the research in Switzerland, so which nation has the brains to construct such a huge project?'

'Look,' said Deepak, 'the Israelis, with the United States, built the atomic bomb, so now they don't want to get left behind in the race for time travel.'

'Sorry, Deepak,' James replied, 'but a half-mile-long tunnel is never going to transform matter into the future. Look at the difficulties Jessica had with that tube tunnel in London.'

'Well, it's not just a half-mile tunnel; the beam is being contained right through Green Castle Hill. That's longer than the accelerator in California. And then it's bounced up into the atmosphere. The problem with you humans is your intense passion for growth. You will have to learn what the *Bhagavad Gita*says: "All is clouded by desire". Really, that's all the advice I can give you.' After a moment's hesitation, however, he continued, 'Look there are dark clouds coming this year, which may affect the Middle East.' James was surprised, as the U.S. president had spent a lot of time on the Oslo agreement. 'James, listen to me. The agreement will be signed late in September, but then the leader will be assassinated by November, and another will be named as the acting prime minister. You know what that means for the project down there; it will only gather more speed.'

With that, Deepak started to fumble with a large blue medallion he was wearing around his neck. 'Oh, I'm really sorry, James. You've missed the time window to return tonight! Now let's see ... the best I can do is same place, same time on Thursday evening. Very sorry, but you will miss two days of your life,' he stated bluntly.

'Look, Deepak, I'm not waiting here for another two days,' complained James. 'You just put me straight back as soon as you can!'

'No problem,' said Deepak. 'Let's just walk down the hill a bit so as not to alert the workers on the farm. There's a bright flash, you see, when we leave, but all will be fine with your return. Really, you can trust me,' Deepak said.

'Thanks,' said James. 'You have been most helpful. But what about the car down there? Will that follow me also?' He pointed to the car.

'Ah! Good point,' replied Deepak. 'No, we leave it here so there will be two cars, and the garage will make twice the profit.' He smiled and adjusted his medallion. As they embraced, there was a flash, and each went his own way.

St. John's Harbour, Antigua—Thursday, 26 January 1995

When James awoke next, he was still sitting on the road in St John's, propped up against a car, and it was dark. A motorbike was roaring down the road towards him, and he dove half under the car just in time to keep from being run over. Looking out from underneath, he could see the whole of Heritage Quay was a bustle of young people enjoying themselves on a tropical evening. James was back in 1995. Trying not to attract attention, he crawled out from underneath the car, stooping down, as if he had been searching for his car keys. He was delighted to see that he was now wearing his casual shirt and slacks again, and the car was the blue saloon Gina had hired. He was not so pleased to see a clutch of parking tickets on the windscreen, which he removed and stuffed in the glove box. Finding his keys, he started the car and headed back out of St John's for the Halcyon Cove Hotel. On his arrival at the gate, the guard wanted to talk to him. 'Welcome back, Mr Pollack. Been away on a trip?' he asked.

James bluffed a reply, 'Actually, yes. I've been over to look at one of the other islands.' And with that, James drove down the drive to the parking area. He suddenly realized what he had said and frantically searched for his map of Antigua. When he found it, he almost ran down to the hotel, collected his key from reception, and went straight up to his room. Placing the map on the writing desk, he was soon able to locate the fruit farm. He drew a line west through Green Castle Hill. Turning the map over on the other side, he found a regional map of Antigua with St. Kitts in the north and the French island of Guadeloupe in the south. Lying just twenty miles to the west was the Island of Montserrat, with its sulphur hills and a dormant volcano in the south.

How could he have been so stupid? Of course that's how they could extend the range of the accelerator. And it would probably cause a volcanic eruption before too long! Feeling happy with his research at last, James stretched out on his bed and fell into a deep sleep. Tomorrow was another day, and somehow he would have to explain all this to his lovely Gina ...

V.C. Bird International Airport, Antigua—Friday, 27 January 1995

James was awakened by a knocking on his door and the sound of a key being turned in the lock. When he looked up, he saw a large local chambermaid enter his room, with Gina not far behind. She ran to his bed and kissed him, 'Oh! James, where have you been? I was so worried about you. Are you all right? Nothing hurt I hope.'

James tried to rise to pull her towards him, but his head felt as if it had been squeezed in a mangle! 'God, Gina, I am glad to see you. I'm fine, just a bit bushed from some travel, but it's so good to be back.' James noticed that Gina was wearing a yellow cotton blouse and long white shorts, with pink sports shoes.

'I came over every day to see if you were here, but they said there was no one in your room. Today I came up to check. So when did you get back, James?'

'Late last night,' he replied, 'and I know most of the story now.'

Seeing that everything looked all right, the maid left saying 'Well, I'll leave you two to get acquainted again.'

Once alone, Gina locked the door and then came back to the bed. She started to undress. When she was down to her undies, she joined James on the double bed. 'Come on, let me help you take your shirt and slacks off,' she said. 'You must be hot in all those clothes.'

James whispered to her to put on the TV and turn up the volume to block out their conversation, but when she pulled off his briefs and nothing happened, she knew James was not his usual self. Then James detected an unusual odour about his body. He asked Gina about it, and she replied, 'No, James, nothing bad ... just a strange electrical smell.' Then she turned him around. 'Actually, you have a sort of blue aura all over your body, you know.'

'That's what I thought,' said James. 'I think I'll go and shower to see if I can wash it off. Relax. I won't be long.'

James went to the shower and turned it on cold to help cool him down. He could feel his knees collapsing, when, suddenly, something hit him full in the face. His astral spirit had found him at last, and he felt better almost immediately. He found his shampoo and washed his hair, and that felt better too. Then he lathered his body with some coconut gel and soon he was back in shape again. He picked up a bath towel and, drying his hair, returned to the bedroom only to find Gina naked with her hand between her legs. She was watching a sex film. 'Oh, James,' she said, 'that looks much more impressive. Are you feeling better? I put this on thinking it might help you to recover, and now you do smell good.' She reached for the remote.

'No, leave it on,' said James. 'Let's see what the professionals get up to these days!' He laughed and, lying on the bed, pulled Gina over on top of him. 'You are definitely the most marvellous thing that has happened to me!' And they both sought out deeper fulfilment from each other.

Later, as they showered together, James told Gina what he had seen down at the docks and later up at the fruit farm. It all seemed to confirm what they had discussed—construction of an early accelerator project. It had probably been designed by Israeli scientists, but James thought there must be other parties involved. Gina mentioned that, after the bank had taken over the fruit farm, the whole area had been re-landscaped, so no one could really see inside. They had obtained permission to build a holiday village, but it came with high security fences, and the development had still not come onto the tourist market for rental. When James explained that it might include an intense radiation beam being projected onto another island, Gina looked alarmed.

They were sitting on the floor of the shower, both naked, with dripping hair, caressing each other, when Gina asked, 'James, who exactly do you meet on the other side, and what does he or she tell you?' James looked at her and kissed her deep with his tongue; then, holding her head in his hands, he asked her to try and read his mind. After a few moments, he asked what she had seen. 'Well,' she said after thinking for a bit, 'This man Deepak is your guardian. He's a short Indian with long black hair. I could see him in a heavy overcoat with an embroidered shirt and funny black trousers. He's very positive and protective, and he's been charged to look after your daughter in Eastern Europe ... 'James ... err, you never told me about this, did you?'

'No, I didn't know about her either,' replied James. 'Look, if we ever get separated and you are in danger, this is someone who can help you,' said James.

The sound of the film continued in the other room, and suddenly James felt that he wanted to take Gina away from Antigua. When they had finished another kiss, James whispered in her ear, 'Gina, I don't want to stay another night at this hotel. Would you come over to Montserrat with me, for a long weekend?'

She nodded her reply with a big smile and said, 'After what we just did, I would go almost anywhere with you!' James went back to his room and started to dress in clean shorts and a polo shirt. Turning off the TV, he said in a loud voice that he had to be back in Geneva on Monday, so he would need to check out from the hotel today and leave for New York later that afternoon. Gina replied—equally loudly—how sorry she was, and how she hoped he would come back soon. He could tell from her voice that she was acting, so he just said, 'We can have lunch on the terrace downstairs at one. Can you be ready by then?'

'No problem, James, I'll be there,' was her reply.

Leaving Gina in his bedroom to dress and dry her hair, James went down to the hotel lobby and saw that his favourite hostess was at her desk. He told the girl at reception that he needed to end his holiday early and check out straight away. Overhearing this, Shoshanna came over to help him check out. 'James, leaving us so soon, how can I help?'

'Well, you could give me a cash discount on the second week, if that's possible,' he asked.

'Okay. If you can wait a minute, I'll see what we can do.' The receptionist prepared his room account before Shoshanna returned to say, 'We can give you 80 percent in cash if you agree—U.S. dollars okay?' James accepted and asked the receptionist to book him a seat on the American Airlines flight to New York that afternoon. To his surprise, Shoshanna came around to face James. She asked if there was anything else he needed. James thought fast and replied, 'Yes. You could try and get the commander at the U.S. base on the phone. I just wanted to say good-bye.'

'Yes of course, the commander,' she said. 'I will get him for you right away.' James was impressed how smoothly it all worked, for those in the know, as she passed the phone to him.

'James, it is good to hear from you,' said the commander. 'Everything okay?'

James said, 'Well, sir, I have to leave today, and thought you might like to join us for lunch at the hotel before I go—that is, Ms Martinat and me.'

To James's surprise, the commander said he would be delighted and that he would be over at the hotel in thirty minutes. They agreed to meet at the hotel bar and wait for the lady to join them. James was into his second beer by the time the commander arrived, and they took their drinks out onto the shady terrace. The girl from reception came and confirmed his flight to New York at five that afternoon as the two men settled down to talk business. Gina joined them just as the commander started his explanation: 'The freighter you saw down at the docks the other night was a U.S. military supply ship. Sorry, but I only got a confirmation yesterday. It was sent down here from a stateside base to supply additional equipment, as the project was not meeting expectations.'

James was not surprised and replied, 'So the heavy lifting equipment would be there to move ... what, additional magnets to increase the power?'

The commander nodded. 'Could be. I don't know all the technical detail, but it appears that our government has been working on this since the beginning, together with local scientists here of course.'

James almost exploded, knocking over his beer. 'Commander, there is no one local on this island with much scientific knowledge at all! The majority of people here are engaged in tourism or work in banks indirectly engaged in money laundering, drugs, or other criminal activities such as gun running to the Columbian cartel. So please don't mention any local scientists!'

Gina could see that this meeting was going nowhere and tried to calm James down, but she also wanted more. 'I understand from the de-briefing we had this morning that this machine can generate a highly intense wave of radiation, which may be bounced off the island of Montserrat, a British protectorate, sir,' she said.

'Well now,' said the commander, 'we do have a bright young couple here. Shall we order?' And that was as far as their conversation ever went.

After lunch, James returned the hire car to the company near the airport, with Gina following in her car. Then they went straight to the international airport to buy their tickets for the short flight to Montserrat. Gina had placed a reservation already, and James paid with the cash he had from the hotel refund. They were due to leave at 4.45 p.m. He chatted to the airline agent while Gina went to telephone her office to say that she would be away for a few days. When she came back, James announced that he had booked three nights at a beach guest house and read out from the brochure, '"This lovely villa is centrally located in the quiet Palm Loop area, just a two-minute walk to the beach and local transportation. Enjoy our beautiful waterfront location. We offer the privacy of villa-style accommodation with spacious rooms and airy en-suite bathrooms, ceiling fans, mosquito nets, and lots of closet space." Just what we need for our luggage,' said James, pointing to their hand baggage.

'And what have you lined up for my entertainment?' teased Gina.

'Okay, listen to this, my girl,' said James, reading again. '"Sit at the bar and enjoy the music, or sit in the open air and listen to the sound of waves breaking on the beach below."'

'Okay, I'll come, but only for the waves breaking on the beach!' said Gina, laughing.

'Yes, and the protection of the mosquito nets at night,' said James. 'Look it's time to board. Come on, you go first through immigration.' As James looked back, he realized he had forgotten to cancel his flight to New York, which was also boarding in the terminal. *Well, just one more 'no show'*, he thought.

There were just six other passengers on the plane, and it was raining by the time they walked out onto the tarmac to board the small, two-engine plane. James and Gina were the first to board and went straight for the twin seats at the rear of the plane. As the plane took off to the east, James could see that they were heading straight into a storm coming from the island of Montserrat. The plane banked over Antigua and started its flight westwards into the rain. As the plane bumped around in the storm, they held hands, and James pulled Gina towards him. Then the clouds cleared, and James could see Green Castle Hill below them. In such a small plane they were flying at a low elevation in a direct line towards the mountain on Montserrat. Moments later, the plane hit more turbulence and James could see the pilot struggling with the controls. Then in all the chaos he heard the pilot shouting, 'Mayday! Mayday! This is flight WI-911, We are going down …' Despite his seat belt, James was being physically pulled out of his seat. He suddenly knew what was happening, but how did they know he had switched flights? He held onto Gina as long as he could, but his body was now half outside the fuselage, caught in the slipstream outside. His last words to Gina were to contact Deepak. Then he was gone.

James awoke with a bump sitting in an aisle seat at the back of the American Airlines plane, which was taxiing on the runway in Antigua. No one appeared to notice his arrival. The hostess was walking down the aisle making the last count before take-off. James stopped her as she approached and asked if he could disembark. The tall, formidable hostess eyed him up and down. 'I'm sorry, sir, but we are just about to take off. What seems to be the problem?'

James replied, 'Look, I think I'm on the wrong flight, and I've lost my luggage.'

'Well, that will be in the cargo hold.' She smiled and then looked at him cautiously and asked to see his passport. Seeing he was British, she went to the back of the plane to check the flight manifest. His name was on the list, and she returned to James. 'Well that looks to be in order,' she said, handing back his passport. 'I see by the stamps in your passport that you left Antigua this afternoon, so what's the problem?' And with that, she walked off.

An elderly woman sitting in the window seat turned to James in sympathy. 'I get the same feeling every time I go on one of these planes. Would you like to take one of these pills to help calm you down?' James was furious at having been outsmarted again, and was close to tears at having lost his darling Gina at the same time. Where was she? Whatever had happened to the plane would no doubt be reported on the news channels by the time he got to New York. When he looked down, he could see he was sunburnt all over his arms and legs.

Chapter 4—Italian Adventure

Geneva to Rome—Monday, 18 September 1995

Floating down, the sound resounds
Around the icy waters underground.
—Pink Floyd, 1995

By September, James was back at his bank in Geneva, working on a number of international syndicated credits, most of which were in default. This was not a situation like the one that had happened the last time in 1982, when several emerging markets defaulted at the same time, and Brazil and Mexico had threatened the whole banking system. New agreements for rescheduling had saved the whole financial system from collapse, but it seemed to James that this now happened to the financial markets almost every ten or twelve years! The central banks were either blind, or the greed of easy credit was too much for many sovereign borrowers. Whatever the reason, it looked as if the next global collapse of financial markets would probably take place around 2008.

It was a bright sunny Monday morning as James left his impressive residence, just outside a small village in the Swiss wine-growing area overlooking France. He headed his car down the hill and quickly joined the Route du Mandement, the old pilgrim way to Rome. It was just after six in the morning, and there was little traffic as he drove towards Meyrin on his way to Geneva airport. He needed to catch the early flight to Rome in order to be at the meeting by ten thirty. Driving fast along the Route de Meyrin, he detected a strong smell of fresh onions in the air, although he had no idea where these onion fields could be. Normally he travelled to Italy the night before and stayed at the Hotel Excelsior, to be ready for a meeting the next day. This time, something must have gone wrong over the weekend, as his Italian lawyer had called on Sunday to request his attendance at a hearing of the Commercial Court in Rome. James was more than delighted to agree after what had happened on the previous Saturday night, when he had met his guardian Deepak again.

James had been invited out to a diner at the Auberge in the village of Dardagny, at the far end of the Mandement in the canton of Geneva. The village was not that far from where James lived, but deep in the countryside close to the border with France. The evening had been a boys' night out, after the summer holidays, with lots of laughter about girls on holidays in Greece and the south of France. Leaving the restaurant at after eleven in the evening, most of the men had rushed off home to waiting wives or girlfriends, but James had no one special at that time and had slowly turned his car for the drive home. The road from Dardagny descends down to a small river, and James thought he would take a back way, on lanes that often cross the border into France and return back again into Switzerland. Down in the valley, a strange mist descended on the road, and James put on his headlights to see more clearly. As he drove up out of a wood, the figure of a young girl suddenly rushed forward, straight in front of his car. James frantically braked, but it was too late, and as he hit the girl, her body was thrown into the air, above the car. He suddenly realized her long legs were passing straight through the roof of the car, and he knew he was seeing her astral body. The car finally braked to a stop, and James got out in time to see the body float down onto the tarmac, some yards behind the car. The road was full of a strange autumn mist, with no sound anywhere at all.

'Evening, James.' It was Deepak dressed in his long coat and beaming from ear to ear. 'Sorry about that. I told Natasha to wait until you had passed, but she just ran forward into the road!' James and his guardian walked back towards the body of the girl, which was still lying in the middle of the road.

'Deepak, what's going on this time? And who's this girl you've brought with you?' asked James.

'You have no idea the difficulties we've had,' complained Deepak, 'now that the Large Electron-Positron (LEP) ring is being improved underneath here!'

James ignored this reference to the large electron-positron collider, and when he reached the girl, he couldn't help but notice that she was strangely attractive, dressed in a gold-coloured top and a short, white skirt. Deepak put one arm under her knees and the other under her body and lifted her up like a straw doll. 'All right,' the guardian replied, 'this time I need your help.' And they both walked back towards the car.

James opened the door, and Deepak got into the back with the girl as she started to come back to life again. James got back into the driver's seat and, as he started the engine, he asked, 'All right, what happened this time?'

Deepak took a deep breath and started to explain. 'This is Natasha Pavlak from Russia. She's going to be your new assistant in Beirut,' he explained.

'Deepak, from what you have told me about the place, I have no intention of going anywhere in the Levant, let alone Beirut!' James replied as he drove slowly down the road.

'Yes, well, that's for now,' said Deepak, 'but you may have to cross that bridge. Let me explain about Natasha first. She was on her way to Dubai where she's engaged to be married. Unfortunately, she got into some difficulties, so as she is one of my charges. I need to find her somewhere to stay for a few weeks. I just thought you might help.' Deepak looked expectedly at James.

'That's no problem at all,' said James with a sigh. 'Except that I don't keep much in the way of woman's clothes at the house right now.'

In the next second, a large leather portmanteau hit the road in front of the car. James slammed on the brakes and pulled up beside it. 'Ah!' said Deepak, 'that will be her luggage now. Must have got delayed, but all's well now.' James got out, picked up the heavy bag, and heaved it into the boot of the car. They continued the journey back to James's house in silence. James pulled into the car park in front of a chateau. Natasha appeared to be asleep on the backseat, but Deepak was very much awake. As they both got out of the car, James started to have real concerns. 'Look, Deepak, does this girl speak any English? And what exactly is she going to do around here?' he asked.

'James, she's a graduate from the Leningrad University ... speaks six or seven languages, graduated in celestial mechanics, and plays the piano rather well. You want me to place her in one of those foreign banks, complete with valid work papers, if you agree?' James looked shocked at the news and just nodded. With that, Deepak took out his blue medallion and started to move away. 'I'll be in touch,' was all he said before he disappeared again in a bright flash.

Trevi Fountain, Rome—Monday, 18September 1995

James had boarded the Alitalia plane for the direct flight to Rome. After take-off, the plane gained altitude over France in order to fly over the Alps. The weather was clear and calm, and James had some breath taking views of the mountains. When the plane landed at Fiumicino Airport, the air was hot and humid, and James hurried to the taxi stand, where he had agreed to meet his Italian lawyer. The two men bundled into a taxi and drove off towards the centre of Rome. James had expected that they would arrive at some important building for the courts, but the taxi drew up outside the offices of a law firm on a rather ordinary street, in the hot morning sunshine. They were met outside the building by one of the partners and his female assistant, who was carrying a black bag that contained, James guessed, the briefs of the case. The group of four walked off together toward the civil court where their case would be heard by a magistrate. James fell in behind with the legal assistant, who introduced herself as Alexei Marino. He was pleased to find she spoke excellent English.

The local Italian court reminded James more of a coffee house than a court of law. Several cases must have taken place already that morning, and both men and women were arguing in front of the bar and in the aisles of the courtroom. The young assistant noticed the look of concern on James's face and told him that most of the proceedings were civil divorce cases and often sparked verbal disputes. James sat and said nothing; he didn't understand Italian and had no understanding of the legal proceedings.

After some time, their papers were presented to the court for the repayment of several billion Italian lire. No one looked surprised or was questioned by the court. The two lawyers made their presence known, and the magistrate asked who had brought the case against the Italian state. James was told to stand up in the courtroom, but hardly anyone took any notice. Many others were also standing, engaged in heated discussion, so James sat down and asked if he had been noted. 'Yes,' said one of the lawyers, 'the papers must now be accepted by the court, and we have registered our legal claim. Now someone in the government is going to have to look at the case more seriously.' James could clearly see how this might work, and the affect it might have on the government agencies involved. Somehow, it might just cause someone to panic, which concerned him a bit more.

As soon as they left the courthouse, the two lawyers summoned a taxi and told their assistant to look after James for lunch. She was a short, dark-haired legal assistant, about twenty-five years old and well dressed in a knee-length dark suit and white blouse. James, as usual when abroad, sported his light brown suit and was carrying his overnight bag on his shoulder. 'So you're the British banker who works in Geneva,' said Alexei. 'What do you think of our city?' Alexei was well educated and intelligent, which was evident as she started to make polite conversation between two professionals.

James just laughed and put her more at ease by saying he had been in Rome some thirty years ago and would like to go back and see the Trevi Fountain, and have some lunch nearby. Alexei agreed and led the way down the Via Lavatore looking in the shop windows. Soon they came to the pedestrian street that leads to the fountain. This narrow street was a mixture of the old and new—luxury tourist shops, and one with new age tarot cards on display. They came at last to the Trevi Fountain, which was surrounded by cafe tables set outside in the square. Alexei guided James to a pizzeria in the corner. It was out of the sun, and there were fewer tourists around it.

After they sat down at a table, James removed his jacket, and Alexei opened her jacket to relax. 'So what brought you to this fountain all those years ago, James, if you don't mind me asking?'

'It was a summer holiday,' he answered. 'Four of us boys drove down to Rome in a blue Mini, although we didn't rob any banks.' James laughed, referring to the 1969 film *The Italian Job*. They both laughed and ordered some cold drinks to enjoy while they looked at the menu.

'Did you throw a coin in the fountain last time?' she asked. 'You know, that often means you will come back to Rome.'

'That's right,' he answered. 'I did then, but I'm not so sure that I want to do it again, or should I?'

'Well that really depends,' she said smiling. 'Is this the life you were born to live? Or are you looking for something different? If you know what I mean.' Alexei was sitting back in her chair wearing a large pair of black sunglasses, with her legs stretched out in the bright sunshine. James was starting to find this girl more interesting as they ordered their lunch.

When they finished eating, Alexei asked which hotel he usually stayed at in Rome, and James mentioned the Excelsior, but thought after the meeting today he might stay somewhere around the fountain, just for old time's sake. Alexei reached over the table and placed her business card in his hand. Then she looked James straight in the face. 'Look, I have to go back to the office now, but it would probably be best if you book into one of these hotels early tonight. Don't stay out late, and if you get into trouble, my home number is on the back of the card. Just call me—I'm living quite close to here.' With that, she stood up, shook James's hand, and walked off into the crowd, leaving James wondering if he had just received a warning or an invitation.

Geneva—Saturday, 16 September 1995

James was in no rush and stayed seated at his table near the Trevi Fountain. He ordered another *cafè* before he left and started to think about what had happened back at his house at the weekend. After Deepak left, the Russian girl had opened the back door of the car and introduced herself to James. 'Hello, my name is Natasha, and I'm really sorry about all the trouble I've caused you.'

'Please don't apologise,' James had said. 'I'm the one who should say sorry for nearly running you over. I do hope you have recovered from that shock.' Natasha nodded and looked around at the large chateau behind them, which was lit up yellow in the evening light.

'Have your family lived here for a long time?' she said, impressed by the size of the building.

'Well, actually I don't live in the chateau,' explained James. 'I rent a small house on the grounds. It was part of the old stables. Come on, let me show you around.' He picked up her bag, and she followed him out of the car park, through a wrought iron gate, and up the driveway to a small converted house. James unlocked the door and ushered her in.

The kitchen was on the right—nothing special, but it faced south so it got lots of sun. Next to the kitchen was the lounge, and down a corridor were wooden stairs that led up to three bedrooms on the first floor. James left her luggage at the bottom of the stairs. 'Would you like a cup of tea?' he asked.

'Oh! I forgot you were British,' exclaimed Natasha. 'Do you have anything a bit stronger? It's been a long day.' She sighed.

'No vodka, I'm afraid,' said James. 'But I have some scotch, if that will do.' At her nod, he went off in search of a bottle and two glasses. When he came back, she was sitting in the kitchen, playing with the tablecloth.

'So you live here all on your own with no woman, is that all right for you?' she asked.

'Yes, that's correct. I'm divorced, and just never found the right girl I suppose,' replied James. He poured their drinks and said, 'Cheers,' to which she replied, 'Bottoms up'. She smiled at James at last. James sat down and started to look at her. Natasha was a tall young woman with blonde hair and blue eyes. *Her arms and legs are thin*, thought James. *A bit like a ballet dancer. And no breasts at all.* Her short skirt showed off her long legs. She had a wide mouth and white teeth.

Natasha asked if the particle accelerator built by CERN went under the house, but James assured her that it existed in a much larger underground circle around them. He was surprised at her interest in CERN—the European Organization for Nuclear Research (In French: *Organisation Européennepour la RechercheNucléaire).* Then she asked why the old LEP ring was being closed down, and James explained they were making a bigger and better one. Natasha thought it would take many years to make a real particle accelerator, and spoke as if she knew most of the principles already. 'In our country they have been studying this for many years, so we know much about quantum chemistry and molecular structure,' she advised.

James had little idea what she was talking about and, after his experience in Antigua, he wasn't going to get into a long discussion. 'Come on, let's get you settled in your room, and you can tell me all about this tomorrow.' They finished their drinks, and James showed her upstairs to a spare bedroom next to the bathroom. He went to find her some towels, and by the time he came back, she was naked, with the window open wide, singing to herself.

'This place is so beautiful,' she said, turning to him. 'With all the trees and vineyards right outside, you must be so happy living here.' Natasha took a towel from James and told him she was going to shower. She went into the bathroom. There was only one bathroom upstairs, and James thought they would have to make some rules if they were going to live together for a while.

He went downstairs, turned off all the lights, locked the door, and retired to his bedroom. James, who slept in a big double bed, usually naked in the summer, undressed and climbed under the covers. He had hardly switched off his light when there was a tap on his door. At his invitation, Natasha opened the door a bit. 'James, I'm frightened in this house on my own,' she said. 'Can I come and sleep with you?' James had little choice but to agree, and she climbed into bed also naked. They lay side by side for a while not moving. James felt he was in a film—a man and a woman waiting to see who would make the first move. James could smell her body; it reminded him of fresh flowers. But it was Natasha who turned on her side to caress his face. Soon she was kissing him and feeling his chest with her thin hands, and then moving down lower to arouse him. Still James didn't move, but let her do all the foreplay. She was well experienced and was having a good effect on James. Before he knew it, she was on top of him and they were coupled together. James held back for as long as he could, but her muscles were milking him to a climax. When he finished, she gave him a good-night kiss and lay on her front with an arm across his chest. She was soon fast asleep.

Rome—Monday, 18September 1995

After he left the restaurant at the Trevi Fountain, James thought he would explore some more of Rome. His lawyer had told him to stay in the capital for another day in case they could get a meeting with the governor at the Bank of Italy. He had never had this sort of freedom before. He'd always been rushing to a meeting or the next flight home. James walked slowly in a southerly direction looking in shop windowsand then he turned north to retrace his footsteps. He had a map of Rome in his bag, but wanted to see where he ended up after a random stroll. To his surprise, he found himself standing outside an impressive villa, with the familiar Swiss national emblem above the gateway. At first he hesitated, but then something told him to go in and ask for a meeting. The inside of the house was as attractive as the outside, with polished wood and engravings of the Swiss mountains on the walls. In fact, it was not until he had been shown to a waiting room that he realized he hadn't a clue about what he was going to say.

He was met by the consul, a Swiss Italian by his height, who was delighted that James had dropped by for a chat. The consul offered James a cold Swiss mineral water, but no tea. James offered his visiting card and explained that his bank in Geneva had been exposed to an international syndicated credit, which was in dispute with the Italian government. He gave few details, but the consul appeared to be well briefed on the problem. To James's amazement, the consul revealed that a senior official had recently opened a Swiss bank account in Chiasso, close to the Italian border, which was now under surveillance. When James explained that his bank had started a legal action that morning, the diplomat looked more concerned. When James asked if he should return by plane or train to Switzerland, the consul suggested that it might be best if James left Rome and 'disappeared' for a few days. He suggested a stay at a resort on the coast.

After James left the meeting, he took a taxi straight back to the Trevi Fountain to decide what to do. It was now past four in the afternoon, and there were few options open to him tonight. He decided to book into one of the hotels above the Trevi Fountain, as he still had Alexei's card with an offer of assistance, if needed. He quickly left the taxi and walked up the street to the hotels above the fountain. He lingered to take off his jacket and tie, stuffed them into his bag, and put on a coloured sweatshirt instead. He now looked more like a tourist. He chose the first hotel on the corner, the Hotel Delle Nazioni, and walked inside to see if there was a room available for the night. At first the concierge offered him a room on the eighth floor, but James wanted a view onto the fountain below and accepted a room on the third floor, with the view. On reaching his room, James threw himself onto the bed and slept for an hour or more.

When he awoke, it was getting dark outside; the sun was setting in the west over Rome. James showered, put on a pair of jeans and his sweatshirt, and planned what to do for an evening alone. He thought it best to go down to another of the restaurants in front of the fountain, eat a pizza, and retire early to bed.

As he left the hotel, he tried to blend in with the other tourists. He threw some coins into the fountain, had dinner, and was back in his hotel room by nine. He watched some Italian television and was asleep by ten. Around two thirty in the morning, James was awakened by the hotel fire alarm and the sound of people leaving their rooms for safety outside. He immediately reached for the room phone and dialled the number on the back of Alexei's card. The phone must have rung at least six times before she answered. 'Hello, Miss Marino, this is James Pollack. We met today. I'm staying at the Hotel Delle Nazioniin the Via Poli, and there appears to be a fire!'

A cool calm voice said. 'Don't go outside. Go down the stairs and find the side exit. I'll meet you there in ten minutes. Look for a scooter.'

James looked out his window and saw that the scene around the fountain looked like something from the Titanic; all the guests were clearly visible—in various forms of night dress, carrying their possessions—in the flood lights. James carefully packed his bag and, leaving the key in the door, made his way downstairs by a back staircase he had seen before. At first he found the door onto the side street was locked, but around the corner was a fire door, which he pushed open. He walked outside into the night air and carefully closed the door behind him. Then he waited. Two minutes later, Alexei arrived on a scooter. James jumped on behind her, and they raced up the street away from all the commotion. James was holding onto her bare tummy for his life as they bumped over the cobbled streets. He couldn't help notice that she was wearing shorts and a cropped cotton top as they made a big detour around the fountain and then back to her apartment. They stopped in a narrow street, where Alexei chained up her scooter. She led him inside an old apartment block. First, they took an ancient elevator to the top of the building and then had to climb another flight of stairs to her flat in the attic.

Once inside, Alexei offered James a cold beer and opened one for herself as well. 'Thanks,' said James, 'I think you may have saved my life.' He explained about his meeting with the Swiss diplomat who had thought it best if James disappeared for a few days.

'What ... was that all he told you?' she questioned. 'Look, James, the top man of the agency was found dead in his car yesterday, after it crashed near the Italian border. He had left Rome with several million dollars, but no money has been recovered. You have probably become one of the hottest people wanted by the Mafia in Rome tonight.'

James thought for a moment and then said, 'Yes ... well, I do seem to get into unusual situations. Now let's sleep on it and decide what to do in the morning, all right?'

'Fine by me,' said Alexei. 'I'll make up the couch in the sitting room if that's all right.' James soon settled down on the sofa and slept with his feet stuck out over one of the arms. He was awakened in the morning by Alexei, wearing a short nightie and offering him a cup of her best Italian coffee. She sat down on the edge of the sofa, showing far more of her legs than a young girl should, but appeared past caring. 'James, what are we going to do with you? If you go to the train station or the airport, you will easily be spotted. Really, I don't know what to do.'

James loved it when girls couldn't see a way out of a simple problem. He let his fingers trail up her thigh onto her bare tummy. Alexei said nothing until his hand started to descend between her thighs onto her bushy hair, at which point she leant forward and kissed James fully on the lips.

Not a word more was said as she stood up and raised the nightdress above her head to show James her naked body. She had a most attractive figure. She then pulled the covers off the sofa and, taking James's hand, led him into her bedroom. They spent the rest of the morning satisfying each other, after which James could do little more for either of them. When they surfaced from dosing together in each other's arms, James thought it was time to propose a solution to his problem. 'Alexei, I know it's September, but would you like to join me for a few days; holiday on the coast, like a newly married couple?'

Her reply was not unexpected, 'James really, you're not married are you?'

To which James replied, 'No, my dear, I'm divorced, but a loving couple would attract a lot less attention than a single man, wouldn't they?'

Frascati, Italy—Tuesday, 19 September 1995

Alexei agreed to James's holiday proposition and went to make the arrangements with her law firm. James went to take his shower. It was already Tuesday, and James was in no hurry to return to Geneva. As he washed his hair under the shower, he thought that a few days on the coast might be too obvious. Why not go the other way to somewhere outside Rome, like the village east of Rome? It would be far more secure. Alexei arranged for an unlicensed car to pick them up later that afternoon, but James told her nothing of his new plan. She went out quickly to buy James some more underwear and a pair of shorts. When she returned, she changed into khaki shorts and a pink blouse, and they were ready to go and wait downstairs for the car. James had written the destination on a piece of paper, and when they got into the car, he gave it to the driver. When the car headed east and not west, Alexei looked concerned, but James put his hand on her bare thigh and squeezed hard, for which he was rewarded with a kiss.

On arriving in the village, he asked Alexei to tell the driver to stop at the best hotel, and they both got out. It took Alexei some time to wangle a room out of the concierge, but at last they had a double room for two nights, with a view of Rome in the distance. The hotel was nothing special, but clean and basic and perfect for their purpose. As the sun set over Rome, Alexei was amazed at how beautiful her city was in the evening light. They washed each other in the shower and then dressed for diner. James insisted she put on a short summer skirt, and he wore his jeans. They both decided to go and look for a real local pizza house in the village rather than eat in the hotel. After wondering around a few back streets, they came across a hostelry that served real Italian food and Frascati wine for a few thousand lire. As they went back to the hotel, arm in arm, James felt he was at last in charge and enjoying himself.

Geneva—Sunday, 17 September 1995

When James woke up in the morning, he was alone in bed, so he guessed that Natasha must be an early riser. It was a beautiful sunny day, and the temperature was still high for the early autumn. James looked out the window and could see that the grapes on the vines had turned dark red and must be nearly ripe. Putting on his dressing gown, he went downstairs to see what Natasha had been doing. From the kitchen window, he could see that she was exercising on the front lawn. She was barefoot and was wearing a tight pair of white shorts and a top that was several sizes too small. He opened the front door and called to her. 'Good morning! And where did you find those ridiculous clothes, may I ask?'

As she approached, James realized they were the tennis clothes of his younger son, who visited him each summer. 'Good Morning, sir,' she replied in a cheeky way, giving him a kiss on both cheeks. 'These sports clothes?' she said, making a courtesy to James. 'I found them in the other bedroom upstairs. They must belong to your children. Is that right?'

James nodded and replied, 'Well, you can see your sex quite clearly, my dear, ' pointing to where the shorts cut into her body.

'James, there is no-one around, and I thought you would like to see me looking sexy in the morning.' James agreed that she did look good, but did this girl move fast. She had only been in the house for a few hours and had already slept in his bed. And now she was wearing his son's clothes! He wondered what was coming next. She quickly bounced through the door and pointed at the kitchen table, 'Come and see what I have found you for breakfast,' she said excitedly. James couldn't believe his eyes. There was a plate of white grapes, red apples, and figs, and a bowl of walnuts. Natasha soon told him, 'I found all this outside in the vineyards. Cost nothing.' James just smiled. This girl was most certainly different, and he was starting to enjoy her company.

James sat down at the table and started to play with the walnuts while Natasha took off her shorts and came to sit on his knee. She put one arm around his shoulder. James was intrigued. 'Tell me, Natasha, how you keep up with all this boundless energy you appear to have?'

'Well, that's simple. It's mostly because of you, don't you know? A woman's body becomes tired unless she gets regular fluid from her man. So what we did last night actually helps me keep in balance. And with the yoga I did outside this morning, I now feel good as well. You really have been most patient with me.' James had become aroused while she was talking, and his dressing gown had fallen open on both sides. It only took her a moment to place him against her, and then he was inside her again. James realized that breakfast was going to have to wait as, with renewed confidence, she pleasured herself against him this time.

They bathed together, after which they dressed in casual clothes for the weekend. James wore a tennis shirt and pair of shorts; Natasha dressed in a short cotton skirt and a matching top. He guessed she wore little else. As it was hot and humid, James said he would prepare a barbeque outside for their Sunday lunch. The best thing about the house was that there was a covered area in the garden where they could sit, even if there was a shower of rain. Today the weather looked as if it would be hot, with a possible storm in the afternoon. Whilst he was downstairs preparing lunch, the phone rang and the bank's lawyer requested his presence in Rome on Monday. James was quietly pleased to go away for a few days and leave Natasha to settle in. He thought he would tell her later and not spoil their day together. When she came down, Natasha was wearing glasses and holding a file of scientific papers with diagrams and lots of figures and writing in Russian. James wondered what she wanted to discuss next.

Taking two beers out of the fridge, he went outside to join her next to the barbecue on which he was roasting a chicken on a spit. Natasha spread her papers out on the table and looked at James for his attention. 'Right now, Deepak asked me to give you some more instruction, as he never has enough time. Now, if you are to survive into the next millennium, James, you need to know what may happen to the Earth's axis in the future. Look what we have found at my university about the Earth's inner core. Recent measurements have shown that this displacement is increasing by two kilometres a year, and if the core continues to move towards the Earth's surface, it will eventually turn over on itself someday!' James was watching the barbeque and the light shining through her newly washed hair. He was having difficulty understanding much of what she was saying. 'The last time this happened was at the time of the great flood, but core samples show that the Earth's magnetic field has flipped over several times in the past, and this could happen again.' She stopped talking for a moment and looked at him. 'James, are you listening to me?' she asked. 'Deepak said you would be a difficult student, and he was most certainly right!'

'Yes. But, according to the theory of isostasy, the continental crust is thick and light, while the oceanic crust is thin and dense, which in effect makes the Earth self-balancing, doesn't it?' said James.

'Yes, but the plasticity of the Earth's interior has another side effect. The centrifugal force from the Earth's rotation causes the crust to bulge at the equator by some twenty kilometres. Changing the rotation of a sphere is hard, until the core moves close to, or breaks through the surface. I've got some calculations here of the amount of energy contained in the Earth's rotation which is large: 2.1×10 to the 29 joules, while the kinetic energy of the Earth in orbit is about 2.7×10 to 33 joules, so only the movement of the core could possibly change the Earth's rotation in a major way,' said Natasha pointing to her papers.

'I'm sorry, my dear,' said James. 'But you are losing me with these details. I'm a lot more interested in time travel at the moment—I need to find someone.' Then he went on, 'I was working with this girl in the Caribbean and we were on a small plane that crashed into the sea. Everyone was rescued except the two of us, and they never found her body, so I think she is alive somewhere. As you can see, I am right in front of you, so I can't believe she died.'

'Well, James, I'm not an expert in this field,' said Natasha. 'It's really Deepak you should ask. You know none of the Hawkins's theories have been proved yet, so even his ideas about black holes and parallel worlds may be wrong,' she explained.

'Yes, that's why they're building the particle accelerator down the road from here,' said James. 'But you've been through these wormholes! The theory works, doesn't it?'

'Oh! That was a dreadful experience,' she responded. 'And it's not even very reliable. My baggage arrived a lot later, didn't it?' she said.

'Okay,' added James, 'it's not perfect because the time zones are always changing. Have you done any research into that?'

'Well, not directly, but you know that the planet has not always looked the way it is today,' she explained. 'Archaeologists have even found a sundial in Egypt that could only have been used at latitude 15 north, while Egypt is located at latitude 25-30 north. Some of the Gilgamesh tablets also show that Babylon used to be situated a bit further north than it is today. Of course, governments don't want to admit it, but the Earth may not be a very stable place. We're probably all going to find that out in the next century.'

James was finally becoming quite interested in these ideas, and he went to get a bottle of the local red wine to drink with the chicken, which was certainly cooked by now. Natasha went into the kitchen and brought out her breakfast fruits, which, with some fresh bread and the chicken, made up an interesting meal. James opened the wine and they toasted each other. While Natasha carved the chicken, James was deep in thought about how to solve his personal problem. 'So you think that the planet's tilt may have been different back in time from the 23.5 degrees of today?' asked James.

'Maybe,' she answered, licking chicken juice from her finger, 'but at present, we just don't know for sure. Of course then Deepak's calculations may be affected by the Earth's wobbles, which is yet another complication for time travel,' she explained.

95

'Look, Natasha, can you think of anyone else who might be of help in finding this friend of mine?' asked James.

'Well, yes of course, the best person to ask would be the pope. The Vatican keeps many of the records from the past, some of which are quite unknown.'

'Right,' said James, 'but I can't just walk into the Vatican and ask can I?'

'You don't have to,' she responded. 'If this information exists, it would almost certainly be held at the Papal Palace, outside of Rome, where they have an observatory.' James's eyes lit up, much to the concern of Natasha. 'No, no, James you can't do that,' she warned, 'it's closed to the public and bound to be heavily guarded.'

'Natasha, as someone said to me recently, you have just explained what you are doing in my bed. Please, if you have finished, can we retire upstairs?' With that, James swept her up into his arms laughing. She just managed to pick up the wine as he carried her inside, up the wooden stairs, and into the master bedroom. This time, there was little finesse to his actions. He didn't bother to take off her skirtand, tearing her blouse open, just wanted to show that he was also a man. After some time, she begged James to stop. Her face and neck were bright red; her blouse was torn off at the sleeves, as they had fought each other on the bed. Her skirt was a rag around her waist, and both of them were panting from their exertions and covered in perspiration. Suddenly there was a loud clap of thunder outside from an approaching storm. Natasha jumped up out of the bed. 'God, my papers are outside!' she exclaimed. James took up the bottle of wine and, apart from a few scratches, thought it had been a most satisfactory afternoon.

Castel Gandolfo, Italy—Wednesday, 20 September 1995

James awoke in their hotel in Frascati to a dull and cloudy morning. Seeing that Alexei was still asleep, he reached for the telephone next to the bed. He looked at his watch and noticed that it was already past eight, so first he called his boss at the bank in Geneva. The secretary answered the phone and put him straight through. 'James, good to hear from you,' said his boss. 'The British embassy in Rome tells me you disappeared after a fire at a hotel in Rome. Also anotherbody was found near the Swiss border in a car, so I assume you are safe in bed with some new assistant.' The man chuckled. They had worked together for several years, and James knew not to interrupt. 'Look there is some good news at last in this whole ghastly affair. The Central Bank has asked for a meeting with all the international players tomorrow in Rome. If you can make it, please give our lawyer a call and just try to be there.' And with that he hung up the phone.

James looked at Alexei who appeared to be still asleep, so next he called his lawyer in Milan. Although the lawyer was not at his office yet, James left a message with the secretary to confirm that he would be at the meeting tomorrow in Rome. When Alexei heard this, she opened her dark brown eyes wide to show she was awake. 'James, you bastard … leaving me already,' were here opening words as she pulled him down on top of her.

'Look, darling, there is something I need to do today,' he said, kissing her face and biting her soft ear.

'Well, James, there is something I want from you right now, and I can feel you are up for it.'

After they showered, James asked if she would get the hotel to press his business suit for the meeting, which he expected she would need to attend as well. She was not sure, but as they dressed to go down for breakfast, he said he was interested to visit the Papal Palace in Castel Gandolfo, if there was some public transport available. Alexei was surprised at his knowledge of the region but, knowing that the

British are always interested in historical places, agreed to ask the concierge.

They both ate a leisurely breakfast, which in Italy came complete with cold cuts, local cheese, andlashings of Italian coffee. James was still drinking his coffee when Alexei came back with a colour brochure and reported that a bus would be leaving in half an hour for the village of Castel Gandolfo. She was becoming intrigued at James's interest. As they packed and left for the bus, Alexei remarked, 'Tell me, James, why you are so interested in the Papal Palace?'

'Oh, I don't know,' he answered. 'What does it say in the brochure? Is there an observatory there?'

'Well, yes, there is a photo of it here, but it says the Palace is closed to the public, so you can't go in.'

'Okay, then we'll just have to have another expensive lunch in the village, won't we?' he replied. They boarded the bus and it rattled off down the hill, first to the village of San Lorenzo and then up the hill to Castel Gandolfo, where they had a magnificent view of the Lago Albano, a natural lake next to the village.

Alexei exclaimed, 'James, this place is really beautiful!,Whoever told you about it? Or have you been here before?'

'Well, it's a bit of a long story, but what does it say in your brochure about the observatory?' asked James.

'Okay, let's see now. It says that the two telescopes were used until the 1980s, and although the headquarters of the Vatican Observatory are still located in Castel Gandolfo, the Vatican Observatory Research Group is now hosted in Arizona in the United States.'

James looked interested and replied, 'Well, we're not going to do much observing today with this cloud cover. Does it mention the history of the palace?'

Alexei read on. 'Yes, it says here that the Papal Palace was built on the ruins of the former castle and partly occupies the foundations of a summer residence of the Roman emperor Domitian. James, why exactly are you interested in this place?'

'Well, it's really the observatory that fascinates me,' said James. 'Let's go and have a look.' They left the bus in the centre of the village, and James set off walking south down the Via Pontificio with Alexei holding his arm beside him.

They walked at a leisurely pace down the long road south towards the palace, with Alexei loving the view and the wild flowers in the hedgerow. Although the view was open to the east, there was a three-meter-high stone wall all around the palace grounds. When they turned the corner, they could see the entrance, with a little piazza directly in front of the main building. As they approached, they encountered a high wrought iron gate closed at the entrance. 'Well, my dear James,' said Alexei, 'that's all you are going to see today. What now?'

James had already noticed a restaurant a bit farther back, so they retraced their footsteps to see what was available for lunch. Alexei immediately liked the place and found them a table on the terrace with a good view of the lake. The patron brought the menu and spoke to Alexei at length in Italian. When he had finished, she asked James what he wanted to order, but James was still thinking of a plan and said he would leave her to choose for both of them. With that, he said he needed the toilet and went inside only to emerge into the back garden close to the palace wall. He sat down and went into his astral body to see what was over wall. At first he could see only the buildings, but then he saw the observatory farther out in the grounds. He also saw a wormhole coming straight out of the observatory and passing close to the restaurant. James was delighted.

He went back into his body and, looking at his watch, jumped straight into the wormhole. In a split second, he came out inside the observatory underneath one of the old telescopes. Fortunately there appeared to be no one around, and no alarm sounded. He thought this wormhole probably had a direct connection to the Vatican. As he looked around the platform, he saw a small flight of stairs that led down to a basement, which might be of interest. He descended the narrow stairs and, at the bottom, encountered an unlocked a wooden door. Carefully he opened the door. He found himself in a huge circular chamber that was situated right underneath the observatory. After a brief search, he found the light switch. When the room was illuminated, he saw a circular central floor with a low wooden barrier all the way around on which observers could sit to watch the central area. On looking closer, he saw that the centre of the floor was a Mercator map of the world, of the kind found in a school atlas. This one however was made up of interlocking metal sheets. Other sheets painted black rested on top, and it appeared that the whole machinery could turn. At first, James couldn't understand what it had been made for, unless it had something to do with showing which areas of the world are in light and which are in darkness at any given time. Whatever it was for, it was a marvel of mechanical engineering, and James was determined to work out its purpose.

First he looked for some kind of control panel, but this machinery looked as if it could be turned only by hand. In the centre of the panel were three cylinders made of brass, like the numbers on a combination padlock, but much larger. Each cylinder was engraved with Roman numerals, which could be rotated to represent specific dates in any year. James suddenly realized what this might mean and started to turn the cylinders to the date when Gina went missing on Antigua. First he set the day and month in Roman numerals and then set the year to 1995- MCMXCV, but nothing happened. He then saw there was a large circular handle set near the floor, which appeared to have been much used. James turned the handle, and the black metal plates in the centre of the map started to turn around. He kept turning the handle until the mechanism made a loud click and he guessed the plates were now fixed on his new date. He jumped over the barrier and walked across the map to the Caribbean. A black disc had moved in right across the Caribbean and grew bigger and bigger to cover most of Europe in a big bulge before receding again towards the North Pole. James knew very well that sunlight did not run across the globe like this, and looked for another explanation.

Finally, he saw more Roman numbers set in the wall, all around the circumference of the map, which referred to neither latitude nor longitude. He looked at the greatest extent that the black disc covered Europe and could see the Roman number *MM* engraved on the outer edge. James suddenly realized that this machine was calculating the number of years a person had to jump forward in time from any starting date. If this was correct, the earliest time that Gina could have safely jumped to from Antigua on January 1995 would appear to be some date after the year 2000, and even that would be somewhere in China or northern Russia, so James calculated.

Feeling pleased with his discovery, he switched off the lights and returned upstairs to the observatory. Once there, he considered jumping back into the wormhole, but thought it might come out somewhere under the Vatican. He was going to have to leave by the door in the normal way. When he looked around, he noticed a white lab coat hanging on the wall. Putting it on over his summer clothes, he walked to the door, and much to his relief, it was unlocked. He made his way to the main palace and found the entrance to the road. As luck would have it, a team of gardeners were cleaning the piazza. Their open truck was parked by the closed gates. Knowing it was nearly lunchtime, he waited, hidden behind a pillar. When the men started to put their tools in the truck, he took off his white coat and ran forward, as the gates opened to let the gardeners out. James ran through the gates and walked quickly back to the restaurant. Looking at his watch, he saw he had been gone for over fifteen minutes. He quickly made his way back to the table where Alexei was waiting.

'Ah! There you are, James. I've ordered the touristic menu, which is perfect with three courses of pasta and some fish from the lake. Does that sound all right?' she asked.

'Perfect, my darling,' replied James who was not going to let his latest find upset their day. He ordered a rather overpriced bottle of Frascati wine, and they toasted each other across the table. As more people arrived, their starters were brought to the table, and it was clear that Alexei was enjoying the day as well. By the time they had finished, neither of them could face a desert, so James asked for just two cappuccinos. When he turned around to summon a waiter, he immediately saw a man in a long coat and knew it must be Deepak. He got up to check, and on seeing the beard and the big smile, he invited his guardian over to their table.

'Deepak, what a pleasant surprise!' said James. 'What brings you to these parts?' Alexei was even more curious how he could know anyone in this small part of Italy. Little did she know what was coming next.

'Well, actually I dropped by to see how you were getting on and to ask how much you have told this girl. Go on, tell her, James, why you really came here ... on the suggestion of your Russian girlfriend in Geneva, wasn't it?'

James's face turned pale as Alexei put her hands to her face in amazement. 'Did you tell her about how you are able to move about and have already been in the observatory over there today, James?' asked Deepak.

Alexei was becoming more and more interested. 'James has a remarkable gift and is able to jump between places,' continued Deepak. 'In fact, he once teleported out of one aircraft and into a jet plane waiting to take off. He's become quite accomplished at it, haven't you, James?'

To James's surprise, Alexei now joined in the discussion, 'Look, I don't know how you two know each other, or where you come from, but James is special to me. He's not married, and we enjoy each other's company, so what's wrong with the two of us having some fun? Okay, he has a girl in Geneva, and I've been with other men before, that's not so unusual these days, is it?'

'All right, Deepak,' said James. 'Let me explain it to her.' 'He turned to Alexei. 'I can move between places, but Deepak here is the one who can move forward and back in time. I was with someone close to me in July when the light plane we were on crashed into the sea, and I made an escape to another place. They never found a body, so I think she is still alive, and I came here today to see if I could learn more from the records at the papal observatory. Let me ask Deepak what happened and if he can tell me where this girl is now.' He turned to Deepak for an answer.

'Well, James, you know most of the story now after your little visit to the observatory this morning. I couldn't get her back to you or anywhere in Europe before the next millennium, and now she's in a close relationship with another woman. You see, James, she's happy in the year 2002, and you should know that women can change as they grow older. They can change their friends and relationships.'

'Well, I think that's all sorted out,' said Alexei. 'Deepak, would you like to join us for another coffee?'

'Thank you,' said Deepak. 'You're most kind. You see I don't get out on these social trips as much as I would like, and I really do enjoy your Italian coffee.' When they had finished, Deepak announced he had to go. He thanked Alexei for her understanding and disappeared down the road.

'Wow, James,' she said, 'you really do get around don't you! Now are you going to show me how this teleporting thing works, or do we have to go for the bus?' After James paid the bill, he took Alexei out to the back garden and explained that, if they jumped back together, she might not remember anything she had been told. Alexei replied quite simply, 'James, just take me back to our room at the hotel.' And, suddenly, they were gone. They arrived together back in their room with a bump. James was laughing, but Alexei found the experience quite frightening. 'James,' she said, 'that was awful! No wonder you don't do this very often. My head feels as if it has been compressed, and I have a terrible headache.'

'Sorry,' said James, 'but I did warn you that a wormhole is not nice. Now let's put you to bed, and you can sleep it off.'

Rome, Italy—Thursday, 22 September 1995

The next morning, James awoke to bright sunshine outside and the sound of Alexei singing in the shower. When she finished, she came into their room naked except for a towel around her hair. 'James, what did you do to me yesterday? I feel quite different—almost renewed—but I can't remember a thing!'

'Well,' said James, 'we went for a big lunch in a village nearby, and you were so tired when we got back, I just left you to sleep.'

Alexei was sitting at the dressing table combing out her wet, dark hair. James always thought the bare back of a woman looked almost more attractive than the rest. 'Did we do anything naughty?' she replied in her Italian voice.

'Not that I remember,' said James, 'but I know you enjoyed the meal.' He left it at that. They had to check out of the hotel and get to Rome if he was to make the meeting later that morning. Alexei fussed around her man. While James was in the shower, she brought his newly pressed suit up to the room and put out a clean shirt and tie. When both were ready, they left the hotel and took a taxi down to the Frascati railway station for the train into Rome. They then took another taxi to the Central Bank of Italy where James got out, leaving Alexei to continue to her apartment. Her parting words were, 'James, if you stay over tonight, please, darling, give me a call.' And, with a kiss, she sped away in the car.

The Bank of Italy in Rome is flanked outside by a row of palm trees, which lend an oriental flavour to the nineteenth-century headquarters of the bank. This Italian Central Bank was one of the most professional and Europeanized part of the Italian state. The Central Bank at that time presided over more than a thousand individual banks, ranging from internationally known institutions, like Banco Commercial Italiano, to the tiniest 'monte di pieta' or savings bank, with a single branch in a small town. All of them in theory had to comply with the strict regulations imposed by the Central Bank, but this meant that every bank would be subject only to an audit every seven or eight years. Since the 1970s, the banks had been important sources of finance for the political parties. The banks also helped to finance the rival empires built by politically sponsored industrialists, in which billions of lire were spent on new plants, channelled through a compliant banking system. The opportunity for conflicts of interest and corruption were, of course, immense.

On his arrival at the bank, James was checked through security and joined the other bankers waiting in an anteroom. His lawyer was already there, and after a number of introductions, he drew him to one side and told him that three other banks had now started civil actions against the Italian state. Finally, with the arrival of the vice chairman of a large American bank, the group was ushered into a large conference room, which was furnished with a dark wood table and high-backed wooden chairs. The traffic on the Via Nazionale outside could barely be heard. An agenda had been prepared, each labelled with the name of a participating bank. After some introductory remarks, the minister allowed the American bank, as lead manager, to make his statement. In effect, the banks refused a refinancing, but wanted full and final settlement within three months. There were a number of discussionswhich James thought would go on all morning, but just after noon, the meeting broke up. James went outside to the inner courtyard and met up with his lawyer again, who thought that this time the matter would be settled. They set off to find the best restaurant and celebrate. 'So, James,' asked the lawyer, 'are you going back to Geneva tonight?'

'No,' answered James. 'After this experience, I think I will check into the Excelsior Hotel for just one last night.'

When he got to the hotel, James insisted on having a junior suite with a bathroom the size of Alexei's tiny flat. He called her apartment, but got no reply, so turning over her card, he called her law office in Rome. After some hesitation, he was put through to her. 'Alexei, my dear, I'm staying at the Excelsior tonight, would you like to have dinner with me? Just one last time?' he asked.

'Really, James, but I don't know what to wear to such a place,' she replied.

'Don't worry; just a black cocktail dress will do. If you wear anything else, you'll get thrown out as a hooker!' he replied. 'All right, let's meet at the hotel bar at around seven, is that okay?'

'Really, I can't wait!' she replied.

Alexei arrived at the bar looking radiant in her short cocktail dress with a red rose pinned to her shoulder strap. 'Good evening, James, I don't know what I'm doing here. Is this really our last dinner together?' she complained.

'No,' he said, 'but it's probably the last time I'll be able to afford to stay in this hotel! Now let's order you a glass of champagne.'

They took their drinks to a table next to a window looking out onto the driveway, which was lined with palm trees and settled down together in a large leather settee. 'So, James, you think you have done it this time, do you?' Alexei raised her glass to toast James in his moment of success. They laughed together, and James turned her face to kiss her on the lips. 'No, James, not here. You know we are being watched by everyone at the bar.' Although it was early, James looked around and saw a number of businessmen looking at Alexei, who, in a short dress, was showing off too much of her long brown legs.

When a waiter brought the menu for dinner, they just laughed at each other. 'Please can you tell him that we will be dining upstairs tonight, if you agree?' said James.

'Perfect,' said Alexei. 'Here's to a happy landing.' And she downed her drink in one gulp. As they got up to leave, James approached the bar and asked for a bottle of champagne to be sent up to his room, and they both made an exit to the elevator. Before opening the door, James turned and pinned Alexei to the wall, kissing her urgently and sliding her dress up to expose her panties. 'James, not here, someone may see us!' With that, a waiter appeared with their champagne on a tray and opened the door for them.

Finally in James's room, James signed the bill, and Alexei was amazed at the size of the suite. There was a large reception room with a settee and armchairs, which led into a master bedroom with a giant king-sized bed big enough for four or five persons. The real surprise for Alexei was the bathroom—all tiled in marble and complete with an enormous bathtub, a large Jacuzzi, and four marble wash basins in a row! Alexei just gaped at the opulence and exclaimed, 'James, I've never seen anything like this before!'

'Well, both our lawyers will have earned a fat cheque today, so I thought you deserved some payback as well.' Alexei threw herself into his arms, and this time he pulled the zipper on her dress completely down.

After a passionate embrace, Alexei shrugged the dress off her shoulders and stepped out of it, revealing an attractive set of underwear. 'Please, wait a minute, James,' and she sat down at the dressing table in the bedroom. James took off his shirt and tie as she carefully unpinned the red rose from her dress and handed it to him. 'This is something special; I want you to have it to remember me by, always.'

After they kissed, James went to find his jacket and took out a small black box from a pocket. When he returned to the bedroom, Alexei was still untying her black hair as she studied her reflection in the mirror. James approached, and handed her the box. 'Alexei, I found this for you today, down at one of the shops close to the Trevi Fountain.'

She opened the box, which contained a gold necklace with a blue stone set in a pendant. 'James, it's beautiful,' she said smiling. 'Really … but why a blue stone?' she asked.

'That stone,' explained James, undoing the clip on her bra, 'is to shield you from all the evil men in Rome, of which there appear to quite a number!' Taking the necklace, he fastened it around her neck and saw how it shone in the light above her small, young breasts. Kissing her again, James lifted her up and placed her gently on the bed, where they would begin the mutual release they both needed.

Some hours later, James awoke and got up to go to the bathroom. He started to run the big bathtub for Alexei, adding several bottles of bath salts to the water. At the same time, he filled the Jacuzzi. He knew that, after intimacy, some women want a bit of private time alone, so when all was ready, he carried her through and carefully placed her in the bath. Laughing, she disappeared up to her neck in the bubbles. Next he went back to the writing desk and found the menu for room service, which was written in both Italian and English. Knowing that she liked fish, he ordered a simple menu of shrimp with ravioli, followed by smoked salmon. Then he asked if they had some Damiana tea—with honey. As he hung up the phone, he heard her calling his name from the bathroom. Pouring two glasses of champagne, he went to attend to her needs. After they played with each other in the Jacuzzi for over an hour, the bell finally rang at the door, and James put on a soft cotton dressing gown. He told Alexei to do the same, as dinner would shortly be served.

Over dinner they laughed about their time together in Rome, the escape from the fire at the hotel, and their time in Frascati. Alexei was fascinated by the little Chinese teapot and the two small cups. 'James, I didn't know you were into healthy things like Asian tea,' she said.

'Actually,' said James, 'I ordered the damiana tea for you. It is a natural wonder plant from Mexico. It's known to be a sexual stimulant for both sexes and can produce a bit of a high for up to a couple of hours. Would you like to try some?'

Alexei looked at James and just nodded with a wicked smile on her lips. James poured out two cups of the special tea. Alexei watched him closely and said 'You know, James, the only thing I do remember about today is a strange Indian man you met at the restaurant, where we went for lunch.'

James was too drunk with love and wine to look surprised, and looking into her eyes, he explained, 'Yes, he was some sort of mystic. We get a lot of these folk in Geneva, wanting to tell peoples fortunes.

Really nothing you need be worried about. 'Anyway, you have all the protection you need now with the blue stone on the necklace.'

'Yes, I suppose so. I was just thinking about it in the bath, like all women do, you know.' Alexei got up from the table and, allowing her dressing gown to fall wide open, came and sat on James's knee. 'James, I know we are both a bit drunk, but sometimes I feel I know you, then at other times you are a dark and mysterious person to me. Do you know what I mean?' she asked, running her fingers through his hair.

'Yes, of course I do. Half the time we men never quite know what you women will say or do next. We are just different, that's all, but we still need each other at the same time.' He gently stroked her soft, open thighs.

'Will you come back to Rome soon?' she asked.

'Well, I've been looking for the tomb of the French artist Nicholas Poussin, which has an interesting memorial,' he ventured.

'James, that's easy!' Alexei replied. 'It's just off the shopping centre in the San Lorenzo Church, not far from where you were today. We can go there tomorrow if you have time.'

Damn it, thought James, *best to enjoy the night together.* At least Alexei appeared not to have remembered what Deepak had said, or her experience of teleporting.

Rome, Italy—Friday, 23 September 1995

James and Alexei left the hotel together around ten. They took a taxi to her apartment, and then James went on to the airport. She had tried to persuade James to let her come with him, but he had flatly refused, promising to call her that evening. As the taxi drove out to the airport in the late morning traffic, the weather was becoming very humid, and James guessed a thunderstorm was building up in the hills around Rome. When they reached Fiumicino Airport, just before noon, the rain had just begun, and James hurried inside to check in. He waited patiently in the departure lounge for the early-afternoon flight to Geneva to be called, but shortly after two, the gate attendant announced that the plane would be delayed due to technical difficulties. Normally that would have been enough to warn James, but perhaps being a little hung over from the night before, he thought little of it. It was not until, at the direction of the gate attendant, he gave up his boarding pass at the gate and went down to board a bus that he thought something might be a little strange. On asking a hostess who was also on the bus, he was told that they had switched planes. James soon saw the plane they were headed for—it was one of the twin turbo prop aircraft they normally used on the shorter Geneva-to-Milan route. James boarded the plane with just five other passengers and a crew of three. He was starting to become more concerned, even before they took off.

As the plane taxied out towards the runway, James could see black clouds and thunderstorms to the north of Rome. He suddenly thought he might be about to experience a rerun of what had happened in Antigua some ten years ago, but then realized the dates were different, so it couldn't happen again. A young hostess came around and asked to see the boarding passes, and as James handed his to her, he realized the flight number was 911—the same number of the flight he'd been on in the Caribbean. James tried to stay calm after all the wine last night. There was something about this number that worried him. Nine plus eleven is twenty ... two plus zero is two. Then he remembered that 9-1-1 was used for emergency services in the United States the way 9-9-9 was used in the UK. James jumped up and started to ring his seat bell urgently. The same young flight attendant returned to his seat. 'Excuse me,' said James, 'but I need to talk to the captain straight away.'

'I'm sorry, sir,' she said, settling James back into his seat, 'but we're just about to take off. I'll see if he can talk to you when we are in flight.' James sat nervously. As he waited for the plane to take off, he took out the in-flight magazine and started to write down the numbers printed on the back. He thought the flight number might have something to do with time, so he started to add the years. No, nothing was clear until he got to the next century. Nine eleven, 00,

01, 02. His extrasensory perception homed in on the year 2001. The result still felt unsettling, and he had no idea what it meant.

The turbo prop engines increased to a high-pitched whine as the plane accelerated down the runway and headed north straight towards a large thunderstorm. After take-off, the plane turned to the east, trying to avoid the storm clouds as it also gained altitude. As the plane hit the turbulence, the safety belt signs came on, and the pilot advised the passengers they would be flying through bad weather until they could get above the storm. As James looked out of his window on the right of the plane, he could see nothing but rain. After another twenty minutes, the left engine cut out, and James knew they were not going to make it across the Alps tonight. The captain announced that the plane would have to make an emergency landing in northern Italy, but omitted to say where. The plane was clearly in trouble.

In all the confusion, James got up from his seat and struggled down the narrow aisle towards the open cockpit. The plane was pitching in the turbulence, unable to climb higher on one engine. As he reached the curtain, the captain came out to greet him, 'Hello, James, I'm Captain Phillips. Sorry, but we are not going to Geneva tonight.' James looked at the man in astonishment; it was the same pilot who had been on the plane in Antigua, ten years ago.

'But what are you doing flying in Europe?' asked James.

'Oh, I came back here a couple of years ago ... thought it would be safer, but I've never seen a weather front like this before. It came down from the north and looks to be going right down the Dalmatian coast!' he replied.

'So why not turn back to Rome?' asked James, trying to keep his balance by holding onto the luggage rack.

The pilot's head shook. 'Sorry, we are well past that option, and with most of the Balkans closed off with the war in Yugoslavia, we are now flying east towards Croatia. If we can't land there, then the next best site will be Sofia in Bulgaria. Don't worry, James. We have plenty of fuel. Our emergency sites are about the same distance as Geneva,' he advised. 'Well, good to see you again. Sorry about the detour, but I'll keep you advised.'

James went back to his seat and thought this latest problem had all the hallmarks of Deepak's interference again.

Chapter 5—Time Travel

Vrazhdebna Airport, near Sofia—Friday, 23 September 1995

Democracy dodders. Ferocious Fascism, cackling Communism, equally frauds, cavort crazily all over the globe. They are all hemming us in ...
                    —The Book of the Law, 1904

The plane flew on for another hour, most of the time in heavy turbulence. The captain made continual announcements on the progress across the Balkan states. He first announced his intentions to land at the airport in Skopje, but it closed to commercial traffic just as they approached. Then he advised they would make for Sofia in Bulgaria, which was a further hour away.

At each announcement, James just smiled, as he could see that Deepak was flying the plane, not the pilot. He started to wonder what year it would be by the time they landed in Bulgaria. Finally, the weather cleared, and James could see fields on the ground below them. The pilot announced they were coming into land at Vrazhdebna Airport, near Sofia, and James could hear the landing geargoing down for the landing. Looking at his watch, James realized that the flight from Rome had taken almost three hours, which, for a distance of around 500 miles, he quickly calculated a slow speed of just over 150 knots, headwinds and turbulence not included. As the plane finally landed, the small group of passengers all clapped in appreciation.

The small turbo plane finally came to a stop some distance from what looked like a very old-fashioned international arrivals terminal. After they waited for a long time, a transport bus was dispatched to the plane to ferry the passengers to the terminal. First the two flight attendants went down to open up the cargo hold so that the passengers could retrieve their luggage. James was the last of the passengers to descend with his hand luggage, after which the co-pilot disembarked, carrying a black document case. Last of all, the captain descended, closing the access door behind him before he joined James on the bus.

Back on firm land, James looked at the sky and could see thunderstorms to the west. The sky over the airport was clear, but with no sunset visible. Captain Phillips approached James on the bus smiling and commented, 'Well, James, this time you made it, although I have to admit it was touch and go at times.'

James thanked him and shook his hand and replied, 'So where are we going to now?'

'Okay, James, let me make an announcement to all the passengers first.' As the bus started off in a jerk, belching fumes into the cool evening air, the captain picked up a microphone. 'May I have your attention please,' he began. 'My apologies for this unavoidable delay. Your airline has reserved rooms for you all, free of charge, at the Hotel Balkan in the centre of Sofia. A return plane to Rome will be made available early tomorrow morning.' A young hostess then repeated the announcement in Italian, but most of the passengers appeared too weary to care any longer.

James was surprised at the old-fashioned state of the airport terminal and was looking to see anything with a date. A clock showed him it was just after six in the evening, but all the adverts were written in Bulgarian in Cyrillic script, which he couldn't read. The passengers and crew were being taken through passport control and onto another coach that would take them along to the hotel in town. James thought the whole place seemed stuck in the 1950s. In answer to the frown on his face, the pilot turned to James and said, 'Surprise! Wait until you see what it's like in town—nothing's changed here since the Soviets left in 1990! Bulgaria has found the transition to capitalism more painful than most East European countries,' he explained.

'But I thought this country was set on joining the European Union,' replied James.

'Possible,' said the captain, 'but it won't happen for a while. You know after the Soviets left, the old Communist Party just changed its name to the Socialist Party, and everything has continued as before—or perhaps has gotten worse. Also, the whole place is run by a number of Mafia groups that are connected to the Bulgarian football clubs. These organised crime groups are involved in all the usual activities including drugs, cigarettes, prostitution, and the arms trade, all run in a black economy that exists alongside the official economy. They appear to have good connections with the Russian Mafia, most of the Balkan Mafias, and, of course, the Italian Cosa Nostra, which doesn't help.'

James appeared to be shocked after his secure life in Switzerland and explained that he just wanted to get back to Geneva. As the coach drove into town, the pilot advised that he often flew across from Rome and agreed to meet James for a drink at the hotel bar. He gave James the idea that he had number of ideas in mind for the evening.

Geneva Jubilee Celebrations—Sunday, 30 June, 2002

James had left his British bank in early 1998, and by 2002, he was the director of his own private investment company in Geneva, with modest offices in Beirut, Lebanon. Stock markets were still depressed at that time, but James had found a number of guaranteed investment products, which provided security for his clients and a reasonable income for himself. Although he was horrified by the 9/11 attack on the World Trade Center in 2001, he was not really surprised at such an action against the United States, after diplomats had been unable to solve the problems between Israel and the Palestine Liberation Organization. Arabs had danced in Beirut at news of the U.S. attack, and some Israelis had also danced on the top of a building in New York. The start of a new war in Afghanistan in 2001 appeared to be going well, but James had read somewhere that only 60 percent of invasions had been a historic success, and this was a country where the British had failed a hundred years before. The world was now waiting to see whether a new war would start in Iraq, a country in which James had some business interests. The die was being cast in a plot that would, at best, destroy the U.S. currency and, at worst, plunge the world into deep recession. James could see little reason that this madness had anything to do with his home country, or anyone else in Europe.

At the end of May, James was delighted to receive an invitation for the Golden Jubilee of Her Majesty, Queen Elizabeth II. This was to be a gala reception and lake cruise on one of the largest paddle steamers on Lac Leman. Similar queen's birthday celebrations were being arranged by British communities all over Switzerland in line with the street parties being held in the UK between 1 and 4 June. James noted that the lake cruise would not take place until the end of the month and arranged his diary accordingly. He had booked a trip to Beirut for the middle of June for some outstanding business and would be back in time for the Geneva celebrations.

Around six on the eveningof the celebration, James drove into Geneva to board the steamer *Simplon* along with a large number of other guests. As he approached the Quai du Mont Blanc, where the boat was moored, he encountered an impressive sight. The vessel was dressed overall with coloured flags for the evening festivities. The weather had been hot that weekend, and as he approached the steamer, it looked to be a perfect warm and calm evening for the cruise.

On boarding the vessel, James remembered she was known as one of the most luxurious paddle steamers still working on the lake. The *Simplon* was completed in 1920. With a steam engine providing a top speed of over twenty-nine knots, she could carry over a thousand passengers. James knew from a previous visit that the boat had two decks. The top deck was open, with canopies to provide shade from the sun. Below the deck was a wood-panelled first class restaurant. He made his way straight up the companion ladder to the upper deck to look for his friends. He was a bit surprised that, although he had lived in Geneva for some ten years, he didn't know many of the invited guests. However, there were plenty of drink and refreshments, so he talked to several groups on the stern of the boat. A jazz band started playing music just before the last passengers boarded and the boat cast off. James suddenly noticed a large commotion taking place up at the front by the bar. The British ambassador had arrived from Berne and was demanding his own table, with, of course, a Union flag. A number of other guests had to move their seating in order to accommodate this request. James was intrigued by the audacity of this action in the year 2002, and was determined to meet this intrusive man.

Hotel Balkan, Sofia—Friday, 23 September 1995

On arrival at the hotel, the passengers and crew checked in, and most went up to their rooms. Captain Phillips motioned at James and pointed to the bar, making it clear he wanted a drinking companion. James went up to his room first, which appeared clean, but far from luxurious. When he looked outside, he could see the square and an access road from the main road—Place Sveta Nedelya. Looking closely, he noticed there was hardly any evening traffic, and he started to think this was becoming a bit of a lost place. James went down to the bar on the ground floor. The captain was there at the bar, dressed in his uniform and nursing a beer. As James approached him, he got up and said, 'Good of you to come down. I hoped you would. Let me get you a beer, and call me Lindsay. I'm a Scot and always seem to be a long way from "Auld Reekie"—Edinburgh, you know,' he added in case James might be unfamiliar with that city's nickname.

'Thanks,' said James. 'I'm from the other end of Blighty—a place called Devon, where it's always raining, and we have a lot of cows.'

They both laughed at this formal introduction after all these years. 'So, James, what do you think of Sofia, from what little you have seen?' asked Lindsay. 'And do you know anything about the old and historic country of Bulgaria?'

'Well, we did study a play at school called *Arms and the Man*, answered James. 'I think it was written by Bernard Shaw years ago … bit of an odd story really.'

'Yes, but do you remember what it was about?' enquired Lindsay.

'Now I come to think of it, the play took place during the Serbo-Bulgarian war, in the last century,' said James, suddenly remembering more of the play. 'Then there was this Swiss voluntary soldier who burst into a young Bulgarian woman's bedroom late at night and carried chocolates instead of pistol cartridges! I think the play was really a satire that glorified something as terrible as war, but no one really understood it for a long time. What do you think?' asked James.

'Yes, it only really became popular after the First World War, but then we seem to keep on having wars, don't we, James?' replied the pilot. 'That's pretty good, what else did you study at school?'

'Oh, the usual,' replied James. 'Shakespeare's *Macbeth* was the best. Do you know "If it were done when 'tis done, then 'twere well it were done quickly"?'

'Yes, go on,' said Lindsay, leaning forward in his chair.

'Not sure really,' said James. 'Something about"We'd jump the life to come".'

'And you do know about jumping don't you?' said Lindsey. 'You do, from what I remember in Antigua.'

James just looked at his lager and said nothing.

'Look,' said Lindsey, 'I couldn't help notice that, after you disappeared, this bloody great bearded Indian appeared, even as the plane was filling with water, picked up your girlfriend, and they both disappeared in apoof of light! Before even I could get out! So, assuming you didn't swim ashore or get rescued like the rest of us, you must have jumped to another place, right?'

James didn't really know what to say.

Finally, it was the pilot who explained, 'Look, James, really I'm here to help you. I was just asked to check the story first, which was why I arranged a meeting for you tonight.'

James was now intrigued and replied, 'Well, I don't think I know anyone in Sofia.'

'No, James, but they want to meet you. Now drink up. We have to go for a short walk outside. It's a lovely evening for a stroll down the Tsar Osvoboditel boulevard, and it's not far.'

Geneva Lake cruise—Sunday, 30 June, 2002

A special Geneva association had been created to celebrate the queen's Golden Jubilee, and with limited space on the boat, it was only for British residents who lived in Swiss Romande. With all the important guests now on board, the steamer *Simplon* cast off and made an impressive departure from the Geneva harbour, sailing out between the breakwaters into what is known as the 'Petit Lac Genève'. The sun was still high, but starting to set in the west and the temperature was still above 25 degrees Celsius, a most pleasant evening for a cruise on the lake. Most of the English ladies were wearing long summer dresses, and some wore a large hat for the occasion. It wasn't long before a band was playing music, and dancing began. James found himself a seat at the tables on one side the upper deck close to the large table that had been installed for the ambassador and where other important persons from the consulate had joined him. James waited to see if the ambassador would make a quick tour of the guests before dinner, but he appeared deep in discussion, joining in the festivities with cold drinks in the evening sunshine. James noticed that a tall, slim girl with red hair was providing the top table with liquid refreshments. He had met her at a lunch some weeks before and knew her as Elizabeth Kilmister. He remembered from her visiting card that she worked at one of the many international organisations in Geneva, and was involved with worldwide telecommunication and a close partner with CERN.

He caught her eye as she went to get more drinks, and she stopped to talk, 'James, how nice to see you! So what do you think of the cruise?'

'Great … wonderful evening for it,' replied James. 'Any chance of a natter with his nibs, up there?' James pointed to the top table.

'Well, they are awfully busy at the moment, as you can see,' she replied, smiling at him, 'but I'll see what I can do.'

'Right. Tell him I've just come back from Beirut. Wasn't he something in the Middle East before?' mentioned James.

Some minutes later, Elizabeth beckoned James to come and talk to the ambassador, who moved to the rail on the side of the boat. The two men shook hands as the ambassador eyed James up and down and said, 'I hear you've just come back from the Middle East, but I don't know what you do,' he said.

'Well, I'm an ex-banker, now independent with my own company in Beirut,' said James. 'I just wanted to ask what you thought of the situation in the region right now.'

'Oh, nothing to worry about,' said the ambassador. 'We're working closely with our allies and feel there's really no problem at all. Look. I was in Damascus until a couple of years ago … pretty hot, but we made a lot of progress on the Syrian-Israeli problem, so you have little to worry about.'

'No,' said James. 'What about the problem farther south? Is there really going to be a war?'

'Well, of course that depends, doesn't it? But it's all in the hands of the top brass.'

My God, thought James, *they really are going to do it!* But he simply replied, 'So you enjoyed your stay in Damas?'

'Yes, very much. The swimming pool was a bit small!' He laughed. 'But, really, you should get over and see the opportunities for new business.'

James thanked him, but felt upset. *Something is going very wrong*, he thought.

After his short discussion with the ambassador, James decided to go down to the dining room on the lower deck and hopefully share his meal with some other friends. He soon found a place at a table with the Anglican vicar and several other friends from his church. The discussion was upbeat about the reign of Queen Elizabeth and a garden party that had been held in the Montreux area earlier in the month. The weather had been hot for most of June, and celebrations all over Switzerland had been a great success.

Dinner on the cruise was made available from a large buffet, and plenty of wine was served. After the meal, James felt he needed a breath of fresh air. Just outside the dining room was a large embarkation foyer, with an open view of the lake on both sides. James went and stood outside where he could observe one of the large paddles rotating right under his feet. Although the sun had set, it was still daylight and would not get dark for another hour. *There is a long twilight at this time of the year*, thought James. And he suddenly remembered shooting the stars as a navigator in the navy.

James was abruptly brought back from his dreams by Elizabeth, who pinched his arm and said, 'Found you at last, James! I've been looking all over the boat for you.' James was quite amused and looked at her closely for the first time that evening. She was wearing flared white trousers and a navy top. *Quite the sailor girl*, thought James, *but she probably wants to know what I discussed earlier with the ambassador.*

He was surprised that she had joined him on the outside of the boat, her red hair blowing in the wind and the noise of the paddle turning below them. 'Well, now that you've found me, how can I help, Elizabeth?' asked James. 'If you want to know about my little chat with Basil Brush upstairs, it was private, okay?'

But, to his surprise, she was interested in something else. 'James, as an active man about town, you've been on my radar for some time.'

My God, thought James, *she's interested in me!*

Elizabeth went on, 'Your visitors up at that chateau have caused our friends at CERN a few problems,' she boldly remarked.

'Well, yes,' admitted James. 'I do have a number of old girlfriends who drop by from time to time, but if you're interested there's probably a queue.'

For some reason that James couldn't understand, Elizabeth kicked him hard on the shin, causing him to lose his balance. He had to reach up and hold onto the hull plate above his head. In a split second, he saw Elizabeth lose her balance as well, and with nothing to catch hold on, she fell off the side of the boat, behind the paddle, and into the lake. James looked on in horror as he saw her body floating down the side of the hull, only to disappear behind the stern of the boat. He raced for the accommodation ladder to the upper deck. He ran as fast as he could past the large crowd of dancers until he reached the stern, where the Swiss flag was flying in the breeze. James pulled a life belt off its stand and threw it as far as he could over the side. Finally he saw Elizabeth bobbing on the surface. She was waving at a small speedboat, which was stopping to pick her up. The only person who appeared to have noticed anything was the British consul, who was now standing next to James. 'Bit of a tiff was it, James? Please don't say anything with the ambassador on board. She'll be all right ... just a bit wet that's all.' He then went back to his table as if nothing had happened, and the paddle steamer turned and headed back to Geneva.

Hagia Sophia Church, Sofia—Friday, 23 September 1995

James and Lindsay walked out of the Hotel Balkan in central Sofia and turned north to join the main Boulevard Tsar Osvoboditelgoing southeast out of town. James found the night air cool after the rain, but it was pleasant, and he could see some stars above his head. At some point, Lindsay pointed and they turned left into a smaller road, Knyaz Aleksandra, that ran parallel to Tsar Osvoboditel and opened into a large square—the Place Aleksandra Nevski. During the ten-minute walk, they had seen no one else on the street, and only a few cars had passed. On arriving in the square, Lindsay pointed at a large building on the right. As they approached, James thought the structure might have been built as an enormous fortress. As they got closer, James could make out a cross on the top of a high basilica and realized he was in front of a very old church. Finally, Lindsay enlightened James as to where they were. 'You are looking at the Hagia Sophia Church, one of the most valuable pieces of early Christian architecture in southern Europe. It was built during the reign of the Roman emperor Justinian I, around the sixth century AD, and is a contemporary of the church with the same name in Constantinople. Bulgaria must have been closely linked to Byzantine culture when the church was built. Think of it, James, the world was a very different place then, and Islam had hardly been thought of at that time.' The pilot seemed to have come to a stopping point in his lecture.

'Interesting,' said James, 'but why have you brought me here? There are no lights on, and no one appears to be around.'

'Well,' said Lindsay, 'the church has some sort of magical powers that have protected it from invasion and disaster. As I said before, someone wants to meet with you here tonight.' Lindsay walked over to a small door to the right of the main entrance and knocked on the wooden portal. Nothing happened for some minutes, and he knocked louder the second time. At last the door opened just a crack on a chain and a women's voice called out, 'Captain Philips?'

'Good evening, Sister. I have brought James to see you, as you requested. He has the experience of the way.' And that was all Lindsay said. Following these words, the Sister released the chain and opened the door. In the dim light, James saw an elderly woman dressed in a black robe. Lindsay fell to his knees, took her wrinkled hand in his and kissed it as James watched in amazement.

The woman eyed James shrewdly up and down and finally said, 'Well, not exactly what I expected.' But she held her hand out to James. 'Come, my child, we have little time tonight.' She led them all into the church, then she turned to Lindsay and asked him to keep watch at the door.

James followed the woman through the barely lit church as she made her way towards the main alter, which was situated at the east of the structure, which was built in a basic cross design. Although James could see little, he could make out a number of floral mosaics as they approached the holy altar. Finally the old woman stopped and explained, 'Sophia represents divine wisdom rather than an historical saint. In this church, Sophia is depicted as a woman who stands above three other women who represent faith, hope, and love—all positive forces in this world. Love and wisdom transformed the original initiates of the Christian bridal chamber into accomplished servants of Christ,' she explained. 'What happened since in Christianity is often referred to as the Great Divorce! Now, James, are you ready to go on farther?'

James could see that he had little choice but to go on, although he was somewhat frightened. He replied, 'If you are sure this is all positive, let's proceed.' His guide led him to the side of the high alter where she went down a flight of stairs. James carefully followed her. The next level under the altar appeared to be devoted to a large number of early Christian tombs. James followed the old woman as she led the way, following a string of lights. Finally they climbed down an old wooden ladder into a third level, which looked to James to be a pagan burial site. It was the old necropolis of Serdica—The City of the Dead, which was how Sofia was known in Roman times. At the far end of this chamber were an open area and some stone benches. Waiting there was the distinctive figure of Deepak. James recognizedhis same long dark coat and his black beard. On seeing his guardian again, James ran forward to embrace him. 'Deepak, good to see you again! I was hoping you would tell me where I can find my daughter Nathalie. Is she still in Sofia?' asked James.

The old woman sat on a bench and spoke before Deepak could. 'Well, to tell you the truth, she's been hidden in a convent, a long way from here.' She wrung her hands and appeared to be quite worried. 'She can come to see you only when she is ready.'

Deepak finally spoke. 'Look, James, we are here to explain to you what we are up against and to help delay them, isn't that right,

Sister?' Then he turned to James. 'The world today is becoming a more dangerous place, and tonight we have the chance to change events—if you will help us.'

'Yes, of course,' replied James. 'But what exactly do you want me to do?'

Deepak pointed to the floor. 'Under here, there is a final level,' he said. 'A level so secret that only a few in the church know about it. These are the old astral ways that connect Rome to the church here in Sofia and on to the Hagia Sophia in Turkey, then across to the Temple in Jerusalem and down to the City of Ur or Babylon—what you call worm holes, right.'

'Yes, I've been in one at the Papal Palace. So what are we going to do?' James asked.

'All right, let me try to explain,' said Deepak. 'In the late '80s your time, there was a man who wanted to make weapons of destruction in the land of two rivers you call Iraq. He built a huge gun to fire shells at his enemies. This weapon had the potential to destroy peace in the region. We want you to come with me and go back and destroy this gun!'

James looked at Deepak in amazement. 'But, Deepak, with your powers in time travel this should be easy,' he said in disbelief. 'So why do you need me to help?'

'Because, as your Guardian, I'm from the future, and as you know, when we go back in time, we all become less powerful. That's why we need your help,' replied Deepak.

James thought for a moment. 'Any idea where this gun is now?' he asked.

'Well, James, it's buried in the side of a hill, close to the ancient Tower of Babylon—and right beside our wormhole. James, this is a conflict between good and evil. Are you with us? Can you help?' asked Deepak.

With little hesitation, James replied, 'All right. Let's do it.'

Babylon, Iraq—Friday, 23 March 1990

As soon as James agreed to help, Deepak led him down some more stone stairs to a huge chamber. A gigantic snake mosaic decorated the floor; the eye of the snake was actually a wooden cover. The old woman took hold of a rope laced through two holes on the cover and pulled the cover to one side. When James looked down, he could see an enormous wormhole. Deepak was preparing to depart. 'From here to Babylon is just 0.3 milliseconds,' he said as he buttoned up his coat. 'Now, we want 1990. Let's try 23March when it's not too hot.' He set the date on the pendant he wore around his neck. James and Deepak embraced and together jumped down into the wormhole. In a flash, they were on the ground in the sand, and James could feel it was hot. When he looked around, he saw Deepak already standing and looking about him. James could see they were in a walled courtyard. There was a wooden gate at one end, but no sight of the gun. 'Okay, Deepak,' said James, 'where do we go to now?'

Deepak was still fiddling with his pendant and replied, 'Close ... very close. Yes, it's right underneath here.'

James got to his feet and saw an entrance on the left. 'Right, let's go and find out if they are friendly.' He quickly ran across the square to the door. Nothing happened, but the door would not open. Suddenly, Deepak was next to James. He grabbed James in a tight embrace, and together, they both passed through to the other side.

Behind the door was a flight of concrete stairs that led down to another level. Deepak checked his blue pendant. 'It's much lower still,' he said. In fact, they descended another two flights until they came to a platform above a huge underground chamber that housed an enormous gun barrel. It was over 500 feet long and was suspended by cables from a steel framework overhead. Huge floodlights were still switched on illuminating the scene.

James looked down in amazement and said 'What in God's name is this thing?'

Deepak replied, 'This is the result of Project Babylon, which is a fairly basic space gun intended to shoot shells into orbit. It might also be fired on unfriendly neighbours.'

'And just how are we going to destroy this, Deepak?' enquired James. 'It must weigh thousands of tons!'

'Well, actually we don't need to destroy the whole thing,' said Deepak. 'We just need one small part of it, you see.'

James looked around and could see that the whole place was deserted. 'Why is there no one here?' asked James.

'Well, the designer died recently, and other people are already on their way here,' replied Deepak.

'How recently did the designer die?' asked James. 'And when exactly will these others arrive?'

'The poor scientist was killed yesterday, and everyone has fled the site, but others will arrive in about ... one hour and ten minutes,' Deepak replied looking at his pendant. 'Come on, James, we have work to do.'

Deepak, followed by James, descended a vertical ladder from the observation platform. It was more than a hundred feet to the floor of the chamber. James looked up at the huge barrel. It was inclined at a shallow angel and mounted on a two enormous rails, so it could be moved outside. Deepak had already climbed up onto the structure and was looking up and down the barrel. James climbed up onto the structure as well and said, 'If you tell me what we are looking for, maybe I can help.' He knew he was asking the obvious.

'Well, it's some form of particle guidance system, if that makes any sense,' replied Deepak.

'That should be easy to find,' said James. 'It should be by the breach of the gun, somewhere here at the back.'

'Yes, of course!' exclaimed Deepak, indicating a sealed steel box on the side of the weapon by the floor. 'Now we just need to open this up and find the electrical circuits, so you can take it back to Geneva.' Deepak pointed his finger at the steel plate. From the tip of his finger issued a blue-white flame that cut a circle out of the side of the box, allowing them access. As the steel peeled back like paper, they both peered inside at an array of electronic circuits. Then Deepak removed what he was looking for. It was smaller than a matchbox. Handing it to James, he again pointed his finger at the box and watched as it exploded into flames. 'No need to leave that for other visitors is there, James?' he said with a chuckle. 'And, look, your American friends will arrive in less than twenty minutes, so we had better be on our way.' They quickly clambered off the gun and made their way up the ladder and finally up the stairs to the ancient ruins above.

Once outside again, both were out of breath, but Deepak went on, 'Now, it's most important that you give this to Natasha as soon as you get back. She'll know what to do with it.' He handed his small treasure to James. 'By the way, how are you two getting on? Hope it's going all right.'

James was embarrassed, but managed to reply, 'Yes, very well indeed. But why does she need this component, and what's it for?' he asked.

Well, the new development at CERN has fallen behind schedule because of problems with the beam. Now this little part is basic, but in the right hands, someone should see how the principle can be applied to particle science. Anyway, it's better not to leave this stuff in the hands of aggressive persons ... who will be at our door, by the way, in less than ten minutes.'

Deepak got his pendant out again and checked it, but James went on, 'So there is going to be a war, here in Iraq isn't there?'

'Yes. James.' Deepak was setting his pendant. 'How about Saturday, 24 September, 2002 ... as close to the chateau in Geneva as possible? There that's all set. Now give my regards to Natasha. Tell her she must be moving on soon. And, by the looks of these arrivals, so must we!' James turned just in time to see three special forces soldiers burst into the courtyard firing automatic rifles, but Deepak was too fast. They both disappeared into different time zones.

Hotel du Rhone, Geneva—Friday, 5 July 2002

The week following the cruise, James called Elizabeth at her office in Geneva partly to apologise for letting her fall in the lake, but mainly to check that she was all right after her swim. She wasn't at her desk, so he left a message for her to call him at his office. To his surprise, she called him straight back, and they agreed to meet for lunch at the Hotel du Rhone on Friday at the end of the week. James liked this hotel because it had underground parking and an informal buffet at lunchtime, which he preferred to a formal meal in the restaurant. James parked his car and walked up through the parking garage to the hotel, where he selected a table close to the bar and waited. A young waitress brought him a beer and the buffet menu. When Elizabeth arrived, she shook hands with James and quietly sat down at the table. She was wearing a brown trouser suit, with a yellow cotton scarf tied around her neck and a pair of short leather boots. It looked as if she expected it to rain.

James took the opportunity to explain that, after she was picked up in the lake, the consul had thought it better not to raise an alarm and the cruise boat had returned to Geneva without further incident. Elizabeth replied that her rescuers in the motorboat had taken her back to Bellevue, where she had parked her car, so no harm had been done at all. James thought this sounded suspicious, but anyone with a name like Ms. Kilmister was going to be cool. He was about to find out she was also more of a problem.

'So, James, how's your business going in Beirut?' she asked. 'Are you going back there for your summer holidays, or somewhere more interesting like Baghdad?'

Alarm bells started to ring in James's head, so he just asked her what part of his business was she interested in.

'James, we've had a problem with this country in the Middle East since the United Nations inspectors left in 1998. We get some odd leads now and then, and satellites pick up some bits of conversations, but really we have no one on the ground to verify these reports. I just wondered if you have heard anything about people buying weapons in this region.'

James looked at her in amazement and then thought he would play her along. 'Well, everyone knows that Sadam has weapons. He even had a big space gun back in the early '90s, part of which was built in the UK, if I remember. He almost got it loaded onto a ship in Hull.'

Elizabeth looked interested. 'How do you know about that?' she asked.

He surprised her when he said that his local bank had done the financing. He pointed at the many banks across the river.

'Yes,' she said, 'but all that took place before the first Gulf War, what the West wants to know is what's happening now?'

James lent back in his red leather chair and smiled. 'I suppose you are going to tell me next that they're concerned about the purchase of enriched uranium. And I thought you were intelligent,' he said.

'Look, you know from CERN how difficult it is to do anything nuclear without a large site and a lot of electricity,' she said. 'So, unless someone finds that, it's just another political scam!'

Elizabeth was becoming more interested. She signalled to the waiter and ordered a small carafe of red wine, which indicated to James that he had her full attention. His ideas were probably not what she had expected and almost certainly would be disregarded, but after 9/11, the West had decided that some Arab aggressor somewhere would have to pay the price. The only problem for James was that they had chosen the one country where he had some promising business contacts. He knew very well that the contractswould be worthless after any invasion, so he tried to probe further. 'You need to understand the Arab mentality in this region. This is a country surrounded by unfriendly neighbours—Iran in the south and Israel in the north—so the ruler needs to have any number of extraordinary weapons to scare off the local opposition. Some think this all looks like a re-run of Pearl Harbor, only this time it's being brokered by a president who wants to show he's better than his dad, and a Fetes public school boy who failed as a guitarist, if you know the players.'

Elizabeth looked at James not knowing what to say, as James went on, 'If the Allies invade, it will disrupt the fragile peace in the region, bankrupt the United States, and collapse the dollar. London, as a financial centre, may well be ruined, which doesn't sound like a good idea to most of us here,' said James. 'But, of course, I may be missing something, like the promise of a secure oil supply and appeasing the Jewish lobby. The government inquiry after will be bigger than Watergate, and David Frost can make another fortune,' said James, laughing.

'Right,' said Elizabeth. 'Shall we order coffee?'

'No thanks,' said James. 'Just a personal opinion from someone on the ground and in the region, probably best to ignore.By the way, when do the tanks go in—end of the year?' James was calculating how he was going to move three million barrels of Kirkuk lightcrude oil before December. Finally, he stood up to leave. Then he thought he was being rude, so he finished by saying, 'Look, Elizabeth, I'm really sorry, but I'm more interested in what's happening elsewhere. If you want to drop by the chateau one evening this summer, just give me a call.' With that James left her to pay the bill.

Geneva, Switzerland—Saturday, 24 September 2002
James at first thought that he was dead and had passed over to the other side. Then he realized he was lying on his back on the side of a grassy bank, beneath a tree. Blue sky was above him, and he could feel warm sunshine. A horsefly landed on his nose, and he knew he was lying in the long grass outside the old chateau near Geneva. His whole body felt dreadful, and he found he couldn't move his head. Looking to the right, he could see Natasha picking up walnuts that

had dropped from a nearby tree. She was wearing a short summer skirt and a white top. James tried to call out to her. On seeing James, she dropped the nuts she'd collected in her skirt and ran down the bank to help him.

'James, you're here!' she exclaimed. 'Whatever are you doing lying down there?'

James was so happy to be back, that a tear was running down his cheek. 'Natasha, it's a long story, but I was helping Deepak, and he sent me back to here. I feel awful! Jumping through wormholes is one thing, but real time travel is most unpleasant.'

Natasha knelt by his side and kissed him on his cheeks. Holding his head in her hands, she said, 'James, I have missed you. Can you not sit up at all?'

James tried to move but nothing happened, so Natasha knelt across his legs and pulled him up into a sitting position. James could see she was naked under her skirt and took deep breaths to try and recover. Slowly, with some more encouragement from Natasha, he felt the life force returning to his body. A farmworker was walking up the lane and smiled at them and walked on.

'Now, James, we have to get you inside. Do you think you can stand up and walk?' she asked. James managed to stand with her help and wanted to pass through the hedge into their small garden, rather than walk around to the main gate by the road. There was a small opening in the trees, and Natasha went first. She jumped down onto the grassy lawn below, while James held onto one of the fir trees above. Suddenly, he was hit by his astral body and fell into the arms of Natasha where she waited below. They both fell down onto the grass, with James now laughing and lying almost on top of Natasha. James kissed her passionately on her open mouth, and she knew James was back again. Now they looked to be fighting, as both tried to tear at each other's clothes. Natasha, being stronger at the moment, pushed James off her and rolled him over onto his back, then sat astride him again. Soon, she had his trousers undone and, as soon as he was ready, she inserted him, rocking him backwards and forwards in the autumn sunshine. Before he knew it, he was spent, and they both lay on the grass out of breath, laughing.After some time, James helped Natasha to her feet, and they both went inside the house to recover. After they showered together, James was ready to sleep, but first he showed Natasha the small device Deepak had taken from the space gun in Iraq. 'It's some sort of guidance system, but I have no idea how or if it works,' he said.

'I'll look at it and tell you more when you feel better,' she said.

'The problem with time travel,' he responded, 'is that we all need protection from the anti-matter. Perhaps this devicewill help,' he replied.

When James awoke, he found Natasha in the kitchen. She was sitting at the table with scientific papers spread out before her. The documents appeared to be about an antiproton decelerator, which had become operational in July 2000. James was completely shocked at the date. All the dates on her papers were in the second millennium. 'But that's impossible!' said James. 'When I left here it was September 1995, and now it's September 2002, so what happened to you, Natasha?' said James shaking his head.

Natasha smiled at him. 'Well, after you left, I was standing by the window and there was a big flash. No noise, mind you, and the Earth didn't move, but I knew I had been moved in time. Everything outside looked the same—the sun was shining and the leaves had started to turn on the trees, like now,' she explained. 'Not speaking much French, and being so close to town, I just walked down the hill to see where I was in time,' she said in a low voice. 'I was surprised to find that it was the same day in September, but the year is now 2002!

James thought for a moment and then said, 'But that's terrible! You've lost seven years of your life!' James exclaimed.

'No, James, having lived most of my life in a Communist state, I'm so pleased to be still here. I showed the authorities at CERN the papers from my professor in Russia, and they offered me a student training with the antiproton project. You see, a woman has to get on in this world today, isn't that so?'

James laughed at how she had few identification papers and still found it possible to keep up with her passion for science. She continued, 'Look, they have modified the AD machine to become an antiproton decelerator—they call it an AD—which slows the antiproton beam from the momentum of 3.57 GeV/c to 100MeV/c. And the beam is cooled with stochastic and electron cooling. James, you don't know how important this is! By the end of the month, this machine will make headlines around the world, with the story of antimatter. The first controlled production of anti-hydrogen atoms at low energy and maybe the first glimpse inside an anti-atom!'

James picked up one of the plans and could see a number of beam stoppers and switching magnets that would keep the beam in a small ring, which leads into the ATRAP. 'So what's this got to do with the small device Deepak found in Babylon?' he asked.

'Well, I don't know for certain,' she said, 'but it looks like this Canadian inventor has found a way to give some guidance to his projectiles. In the past he's had the same problems they had here with the beam. Wasn't this a part of High Altitude Research Project—they called it HARP—funded by the U.S. government?'

'So exactly how large is this decelerator, and where is it in the complex?' asked James.

'Well, it's quite small and mainly underground. The AD team are all young physics graduates from leading universities like Harvard, York University, and some institute in Germany. In fact, I think one of the German boys is in love with me,' Natasha explained.

'Excellent,' said James, 'then can you get us access to this machine tomorrow night, and we can try out this small device I have,' he said.

'James, that would be most inappropriate, but it may just be possible,' replied Natasha.

James thought this would be an excellent opportunity, and asked Natasha to look on the plans to see where the device might improve the current configuration.

Research laboratory—Sunday, 25 September 2002

James and Natasha spent most of Sunday morning in bed, making up for lost time and playing with each other. James asked her in more detail about the AP lab and how the anti-hydrogen trap actually worked. Natasha had spent only a week at the laboratory, and James was amazed at how well she understood the project. 'One of the difficulties,' she explained, 'in making antimatter is the energy the antiprotons possess when they are first made, shooting out close to the speed of light. That's a lot faster than you can shoot at me, James, although you do like to spread your semen in my hair!' She laughed at him. James pinned her arms to the bed and started to bite her on the neck until they both fell into each other's arms again.

Finally, James asked her to go on with the lesson. 'ATRAP was the first to use cold positrons to cool antiprotons. The two ingredients were combined in the same trap, and when they reached the same temperature, some combined to form atoms of anti-hydrogen. They think this may have a practical use in machines for cancer research, so this is where scientific research will help medical treatment in the future.' She rolled away from James and got off the bed. 'Come on,' she said, 'really it's time we got up. I have to call Boris.'

'Boris?' said James. 'He's your German boyfriend at the AP lab, right?'

'No, don't get jealous,' she teased. 'He's just a colleague, but he is our key if you want some help tonight.'

The weather had changed. It was cool and cloudy, so they both dressed in jeans and sweatshirts. Natasha wore an attractive silk scarf to cover the love bite on her neck. James insisted this was to keep other men away, for which she bent his arm again. Her call to Boris had been positive, and they all met for a pizza in a village nearby for lunch. When Natasha showed Boris the device and asked where it had come from, she told him the truth. 'My friend, James here, stole it from the HARP project, and we thought it might have some use with particle guidance,' she explained. Boris appeared to know all about HARP. "That inventor was brilliant,' he said. 'Basically it's the old V3 technology developed in the 1940s. It's not accurate, but could be very scary. The U.S. was not interested because it lacked guidance, but many think he had partly solved this, or would soon if he had not been killed.' Boris was on duty at the laboratory that afternoon and said he would try to test it. He suggested they stop around nine in the evening to see what progress had been made. The laboratory was usually quiet on a Sunday, but it closed at eleven.

Later that evening, James and Natasha went out to the car just before nine, as it was starting to get dark. They drove down to the Mandement and turned left at the traffic lights going towards the French border. As they drove along, James told Natasha that Deepak said she would have to move on soon. Natasha was not happy at the news, and moved up close to James and said, 'I can't stay even if you bite me on the other side?' She let her hand fall onto his knee.

'No, Natasha. Look, as soon as this project is reported, the press will be all over it. Someone in Russia is going to see where you're working, and then questions will be asked. You know your future is in the Middle East, and I will be travelling to Beirut regularly, so we can see each other again, quite soon.'

There was no reply from Natasha. She put her head on James's shoulder and looked ahead and they approached the lights of what would become the world's largest particle accelerator.

The two entrances to this large complex were just before the border, but Natasha told James to continue and turn into a small entrance, just before the Douane—the French customs and excise agency. The road continued across a field of sweet corn under the watchful eyes of guards in a high-security tower and finally came to an entrance on the edge of the site. They both got out and walked down the drive towards what looked like a large underground bunker. James could smell the autumn in the evening air. There was a low mist all around the surrounding trees. When they went inside, there encountered a 30 metre ring built out of metre-thick concrete. Everywhere there were warning signs about radiation. James followed Natasha down to the next level where a glass control room was positioned just above the ring. Natasha waved at Boris and entered the control room, followed by James. Boris was excited at his latest discovery and jumped up to greet them. 'I don't know where you got this gizmo from, but we've scanned its properties and run a simulation on the equipment here, and the first indications are quite staggering. We can see it's not from HARP, is it?' he asked, looking at James.

'No,' said James, 'it was given to me by someone in the Middle East. It's from the early '90s—mean anything to you?'

The face of Boris lit up as he replied, 'My God, this came from Project Babylon—the space gun they were working on before the Gulf War?' James just nodded.

'Right, we're just finishing the second simulation, which will save all the details on our computer. Then you can have it back,' said Boris. 'It may have saved us a couple of years work, and some of the principles can be applied to the Large Hadron Collideras well. Quite amazing,' he went on. After checking some screens for the final download, Boris went outside to retrieve the piece from the R/F equipmentand thenhanded the component back to Natasha. James shook hands with Boris and walked back up the metal stairs to the entry platform. Before Natasha could reach the top of the staircase, the sinister figure of woman dressed in black appeared on the stairs, blocking her way. 'I'll take that, thank you,' she barked, holding out her hand to Natasha in a menacing way.

'Good evening, Elizabeth, and what brings you to this place on a Sunday evening?' said James, pushing his way past Natasha to protect her. He spoke calmly to Natasha, 'This is Miss Kilmister, who has no authority here because security here is run by neither the Swiss nor French police, is it Elizabeth?'

'Y—you two know each other?' stammered Natasha. But then the outer doors blew open and a cold mist descended on the upper platform. Both James and Natasha crouched down on the metal stairway as, finally, the large figure of an Indian in a black coat appeared from the fog. He reached down to Natasha and, taking the device from her hand, turned to Elizabeth and said, 'Actually, this belongs to me.' Then he tucked Natasha under his arm, and they both disappeared into the night. *Deepak*, thought James, *is always there when you need him most!* On reaching the top of the stairs, he helped Elizabeth to her feet and asked if she was all right. Regaining her composure, she asked James who the woman and the bearded Indian were, and where had they gone.

'Oh! I think they've left for the night, Elizabeth. In fact I don't expect to see them for quite a few years.' He then realized that he was going to be lonely at the chateau for a very long time.

Chapter 6—The Final Test

Divonne, France—March 2006

The only thing necessary for the triumph of evil is for good men to do nothing.

—Edmund Burke, 1774 to 1780

James was swimming lengths in the pool at the Centre Valvital in the heart of Divonne-les-Bains in France, close to the Swiss border and twenty minutes from Geneva. He enjoyed coming to this spa on a weekday afternoon as it was generally quiet and a good opportunity to exercise in the refreshing water, which was perfectly pure. The Spa water was heated to a temperature of 37 degrees Celsius for medical requirements, while the pool was a pleasant +30 degrees. Inside, the air was warm and humid as James continued to swim up and down in the clear water. Outside, spring still had yet arrived, as a cold east wind was blowing ... a reminder of winter. Normally the pool was empty, but today there were a number of young school children playing at the side of the pool and getting in his way. James realized it must be the school half term holidays as yet another boy swam into his path.

When he came to a stop at the far end of the pool, he looked around only to see he was next to a young girl who was laughing at him. 'Sorry,' she said in English. 'I'm supposed to be looking after that one.' She pointed to one of the rowdy boys. 'He's a bit of a handful.'

'That's okay,' replied James. 'What's your name?' he asked her directly.

'My name's Nathalie Boyana. I just arrived here in France from Bulgaria,' she replied giving James a broad smile on her bright round face.

James's heart raced as he tried to figure out who she reminded him of. He suddenly realized he had been looking at her for too long without any reply. 'Oh, sorry,' he finally blurted out. 'I'm James, one of those expat Brits … been living in Switzerland for quite a while,' he ventured.

'Well, James, if you want a chat, I'm going to the hammam to warm up after this swim.' And that was all she offered him. James watched as she swam over to the side of the pool and pulled her body out of the water. She had a young figure, and was wearing a one-piece bathing costume. She looked to James to be about twenty-five years old. With her hair covered by plastic bath cap, it was difficult to tell … but he found himself wondering if she was his daughter.

James followed Nathalie out of the pool, past the large Jacuzzi with its mushroom fountain, and up the stairs to the entrance to the solarium and the hammam. The hot steam room was lit only by tiny lights in the roof, which was decorated all over with blue mosaic. There were two levels of wooden seats all around. Sitting on the upper level was the girl. Now, without her bath cap, he could see her long, red hair, which reached down below her shoulders. James carefully arranged his towel on the lower bench not far from the girl, sat down, and waited for her to speak. 'I understand you knew my mother.' That was all she said. James looked at her carefully though the mist and didn't know what to say. The girl went on, 'It's all right. They reconstructed me mostly from my mother's DNA, with maybe just a very small part from you. So, technically, I'm not really your daughter.'

James sighed in relief and replied, 'They can do that now can they?'

'James, we can do a lot of things from where I come from,' she replied. 'As your guardian Deepak has told you, I spent the first twenty years of my life living in a convent in Bulgaria, and you never came to see me. Have you made any progress since you last met Deepak, James?' She smiled.

Suddenly, they heard the sound of someone trying to open the door of the hammam, at which Nathalie raised her hand, and the door locked shut again. The visitor quickly left—in surprise, James suspected. James turned and looked at Nathalie squarely in the face, 'So, Nathalie my dear, what are we here to talk about?' he asked.

'That's very simple,' she said. 'I'm here to change the future. That's all I want to do.'

James continued to look at her full in the face. 'You know we are not allowed to interfere with the future,' he replied. 'Anyway, with the time zones continually changing location, it's really not possible, even if you wanted to.' He spoke with more authority at last.

Nathalie looked at him closely. Perspiration was now running down her face, and she wiped her forehead with her towel as she thought. Then she spoke. 'James, I spent a lot of time studying our country's old papers while I was at the convent in Samokov. Most of the documents were from the nineteenth and twentieth centuries. They were part of the economic collection from the university in Sofia, and were moved to the convent to keep them from being destroyed by the Communists. You should understand that I was shocked by what I read.'

James was now becoming more interested in this girl.

'Haven't you realized anything wrong with our modern finance system, after all your years of experience in Banking?' she asked.

James thought for a moment, taking his towel to rub the sweat from his face and replied, 'Yes, of course, apart from the abundant corruption, we keep on having wars we can't afford, but otherwise we now have some form of monetary union here in Europe.'

Nathalie looked at him sceptically and replied, 'Yes, but we had that in 1866 with the Latin Monetary Union, which Bulgaria joined. Unfortunately, it all fell apart after the Great War, so don't expect the Euro to last for too long either. The reason is that, long before that time, most major European powers raised money for their wars by printing money. This goes right back to Napoleon, who used the major banking families in Europe to finance his military campaigns. Regrettably, the bankers financed both sides of the wars, so as they got richer, the people and whole nations got poorer,' she explained.

James absorbed her detailed knowledge in some wonder and replied, 'Well, yes, that may have happened centuries ago, but with our modern system of central banks today, the World Bank and the International Monetary Fund, global financial markets are protected, so a major financial crash is a thing of the past.'

Nathalie looked at him in some surprise. 'Look, James, you have to go back and look at the history. I studied international relations at the American University in Sofia ... well, online of course at the convent, but you've only got to look at the history of the U.S. Federal Reserve to see how it has all gone astray. Sometimes you learn more if you are not involved in Main Street,' she replied.

'Sure,' said James, 'but that's an old conspiracy theory about the seven most powerful men. It was explained in the book *The Creature from Jekyll Island* byG. Edward Griffin. They wanted to carve out a new system of Reserve Banks, but it didn't happen. It was a Republican idea, but they lost the election in 1912, and a Democrat president insisted on a publicly appointed Federal Reserve Board. Only one member of that original duck shoot got on the first board of the Federal Reserve and that was someone from a European banking dynasty; all the others were independently appointed.' James was proud of his knowledge of banking history.

'Exactly, James, but that was the problem,' countered Nathalie. 'The original idea of the Federal Reserve was based on the European model of a central bank. They really didn't have anywhere else to look, and time was running out, as hostilities in Europe soon erupted into another war.'

James could see where this was going: she was about to explainhow central banks printed money to pay for wars.

But, no, Nathalie thought there was much more to this. 'You see, James, nearly a hundred years later we are talking about a path-dependent world. Path dependency explains how decisions faced by a nation are limited by the decisions made in the past, even though the circumstances may no longer be relevant. In some ways the choices we make today are determined by the paths we have taken in the past. Now you can see why history matters. Our economic future is more and more a product of the political choices we made in the past. There are few good choices left, and many nations, like the United States and the UK, are left with choosing the best of a number of bad options.'

James looked at her again. 'So you can see where we are going in the future? Like Deepak can?' he asked.

Nathalie replied in a cool manner, 'In the short term, yes. There will be another war in the Middle East this year, followed by a world recession, but there are still a lot of variables to be decided,' she replied.

James quickly realized there was a question to all this and asked, 'So what is it that you want me to do?'

The reply came immediately. 'I'm sure you are going to Beirut this summer. Go and find that Russian girl, Natasha Pavlak. You were friendly with her in the past. I should warn you, she is married now, but she's working on an interesting project with the university in the south of the country and has something that may surprise us both.'

James shook his head. 'Look, I'm not wasting my time on some archaeological dig in the south of Lebanon. It's too dangerous.'

Nathalie smiled at him. 'So you two have kept in touch, haven't you?'

'Well, yes, of course. She's been an investment client,' he retorted. 'Anyway, what's your sudden interest in archaeology? I thought you were more inclined to particle accelerators.'

'Well, since you have met my mother, you know that she came from the future. Now I want you to look more closely at life in the past.

If life started more than once on Earth, we can be fairly certain that the rest of the universe is also inhabited. Don't worry about that, James, just let Natasha do the thinking for you. I'm sure you will be much more interested in her long legs, won't you?'

James was ready to slap her face, but then thought better of it and asked, 'So what's your interest in this, Nathalie?' and to his surprise got a reply.

'There are only two counties that have such an extra-terrestrial programme at present, America and Italy. And you do like going to Rome, don't you, James?' He saw their discussion was coming to an end. 'Now, James, we must be getting back to our children. One last thing: make sure you leave Lebanon by the middle of July, as, after that, bad things may happen, understand?' With that, she stood up and, holding the white towel to her chest, started to walk straight through the wall of the hammam! James got up and tried in vain to open the door. 'Oh, for goodness sake, James, do hurry up!' she said releasing the catch from the outside. 'I see you still need Deepak to keep an eye on you. I'll say good-bye outside, if that's all right.' And with that Nathalie was gone.

American University of Beirut—Wednesday, 28 June 2006

Having found a parking space in Hamra, James was walking down the Rue Jeanne d' Arc towards Bliss Street and the American University of Beirut, or AUB as it was known locally. He had arrived in Lebanon on Monday and was eager to get started on his search for Natasha. If she was involved with some archaeology dig at the AUB, then the best place to look would be at the students' union office; they might know where to find her. James was excited at the prospect of meeting Natasha again and quickened his pace. It was eleven in the morning. Bright, hot sunshine was beating down on the pavement. James guessed the temperature was well over 30 degrees Celsius as he arrived at the main gate, the impressive entrance to the university campus. He had been to the university several times before, when his company had hired sales assistants to promote the investment funds they were selling in the Middle East market. Students, he found, were always short of cash, and as it was a private university, the fees at the AUB were not cheap. James walked in through the main gate and turned to his left to follow the path past Ada Hall and the student cafeteria. Then he continued straight on towards West Hall. As he walked along, he smiled at the young students already leaving lectures. The scene was lovely—girls in tight jeans and the university gardens in full flower. West Hall was built in 1914 and still housed the administration offices. It had been, in the past, a centre for recreational activities such as billiards and bowling in the basement, but now the students preferred to sit around talking and playing cards.

James went up the steps at the front and entered West Hall. A double staircase led up to the administration offices on the first floor. James blinked in the shade after the bright sunlight and went up the staircase on the left. There at the top, with her back to James, was Natasha, standing at the window of the administration office. She was wearing an old khaki shirt and shorts. Her desert boots laced up her long legs, and with her blonde hair, she looked even more attractive than before. She turned just as James reached the window and looked in disbelief at James, dressed in his open shirt and safari jacket. 'My God,' she exclaimed. 'It must be Lawrence of Arabia, the only Englishman who visits Lebanon, but never came to see me. Now what are you doing here?'

James loved the way her lips moved as she spoke in English, still with her Russian accent. Kissing her on both cheeks, he replied, 'Hello, Natasha. Actually, I was looking for you.' James leaned against the wall and placed his shoe against her right boot. This caused her to blush, as the clerk behind the window was becoming bored with James's intrusion. 'Well, James, you are just in time to sign up for our dig tomorrow. Do you have your passport with you?' Seeing that he had little choice, he handed over his well-worn passport to the woman in the office, who was surprised at all the visas.

'I see you come to Lebanon a lot,' said the clerk. 'What exactly is your line of business here?'

'My company has an office in Beirut, for finance and investment,' James replied.

'Good,' said the woman. 'That will be $100. I take it you are an amateur in the field of archaeology?'

Before he could reply, Natasha remarked, 'Yes, sadly he is a complete amateur, but I will be taking good care of him.' She smiled at James. James paid the money, took his receipt, and the two of them went downstairs. James looked at the receipt. On it was written, 'Tell el-Burak Archaeology Project—admit one—visitor'.

Outside, they both stopped at the top of the steps and looked at each other. 'Natasha, we have to keep our relationship on a professional basis, now we are married.'

James could see a wicked smile spread across her face, and suddenly she grabbed the lapels of his jacket and forced a French kiss on his open mouth. 'James, you are only the second good thing to have happened to me in the last five years. Where the hell have you been all this time?'

James thought for a moment and replied, 'So what was the first good thing?'

'Having my son,' was the reply. 'Now let's go to the cafeteria and get a cool drink.'

After the initial shock of seeing each other again, they tried to settle down in a corner of the cafeteria, away from gaze of young students. Having got through the initial pleasantries of how they had first met and their guardian Deepak, James asked about her interest in the current project and asked where it was exactly. At this point, Natasha's eyes lit up and she pulled a map out of the knapsack she had been carrying. 'The location of the dig is right here,' she said pointing at spot on a relief map of the area marked Tell Burak. 'It's right on the coast now, although they think the level of the Mediterranean may be higher now than it was in the past.'

'James looked at the topography of the region and quickly saw that the Litani River flowed around a hill, right behind the village of Nabatiye, at the head of a Wadi. 'Hmm, that's interesting,' said James. 'I think we have some driving to do, unless we can find a road up to this village.'

Natasha was leaning forward in her excitement now. She placed both her hands on his knees under the table and looked around before saying in a low voice, 'James, we are finding things at this site that shouldn't be there, don't you understand?'

'Yes, that's what I was told,' he responded. 'I'm just trying to understand why a Bronze Age mud hut might have been so important, that's all. Also there's something wrong with this map today, or the region didn't look like this in the distant past.' he said mysteriously.

'So you'll come and join me at our dig tomorrow, will you James?' she asked.

'Wouldn't miss it, now I've paid my hundred bucks,' he said, laughing. 'Can you drive me down there tomorrow?' They got up to leave and began their walk back to the main gate. Natasha offered to pick him up at the Martyrs car park, in the centre of Beirut, at ten the next morning. They gave each other a kiss, and as James was walking towards the gate, Natasha shouted at him, 'What date are you leaving?'

James waved and replied, 'We have plenty of time … not until the middle of July.'

Tell el-Burak, South Lebanon—Thursday, 29 June 2006

James drove into town the next morning, wearing cotton slacks, boots, and a safari jacket. He passed the Beirut museum and drove down to the new centre of Beirut called the Martyrs Place. This area had been levelled after the civil war to provide a large central square, now planted with new trees, but little else. The huge open space was named after the rebels who were executed by the Turks in 1915. Some remains of the old opera house and the bronze martyr's statue were the only features left of the old Place des Martyrs, originally built under the French mandate. The statue, riddled with bullet holes, had become a symbol for all that was destroyed during the fighting. James recalled that, in 2005, this square witnessed the Cedar Revolution, when a huge public demonstration with thousands of Lebanese people celebrated the withdrawal of Syrian troops from Lebanese territory. James stopped at several traffic lights now operating in the centre of town, as he found his way past a new mosque, which would bring this large, unused space back to its old splendour. Next to the square was an open car park which he had used many times when visiting the nearby Virgin megastore. He had arranged to meet Natasha here and take her car down south to the dig, while he parked his car for a few thousand Lebanese pounds. As it was early, James found a place close to the car park gate and waited for Natasha to arrive. Just before ten, a white Clio entered the park and drove towards James.

Locking his car, James walked over and joined Natasha in her car. She was wearing a white blouse and a khaki skirt that covered her knees, with a pair of dark sunglasses. Natasha smiled as he took off her glasses and kissed her fully on the lips. Her blonde hair smelled of flowers as she pulled away. 'James, not here. We're in a public place. Got your kit and some ID? We're sure to be stopped by the army down there.' James nodded and placed his small bag, which also contained some water, on the floor. Slowly he allowed his hand to rest on the cotton fabric of her skirt between her legs. Natasha smiled in approval. 'You don't change, do you? I brought us a picnic so we don't have to spend the whole day at the dig.' She pointed to a basket on the back seat. 'We can take a break, and go and explore the area and find somewhere quiet on our own if you like.'

James smiled at her and replied, 'Sounds good to me. Let's go.' And with that, she drove out of the car park and back up the hill towards the main road south. They soon drove past the new international airport and continued on the new highway towards Sidon, which took them on down to the old biblical town of Tyre. James looked in the glove compartment to see if there was a road map at the bottom amongst an assortment of tissues. He pulled out an old route map, which had come from one of the local gas stations. 'Oh!

We don't need that,' said Natasha. 'I know the way to Tell Burak by heart. We turn off just after Sidon and take the coast road down to the village of Addusiyye; it's probably not on that map, but it's just north of the present-day village of Sarafond. That was the site of another important Phoenician city called Sarepta, also from the late Bronze Age. You see, this region has been lived in for about 3,500 years.' James took out his pen and marked a cross on the map where Natasha had indicated and saw there was a road going east, into the hinterland and the village of Nabatiye. Then he lent back in his seat and watched the countryside flash by, with an occasional view of the sea. With the sun shining, it was going to be another hot day.

Almost as soon as they turned off the motorway, they ran straight into an army road check, with the Lebanese flag flying from a makeshift post. 'It's all right,' said Natasha. 'They look like soldiers from the regular Lebanese army. Shouldn't be a problem, if you can pass me your ID.' James delved into his bag and handed over his passport. The soldiers were sitting under the shade of a military tent and hardly looked up as the car approached. A guard signalled for the car to stop, and Natasha wound down her window. With their ID in her lap, she smiled and said, '*Marhaba*'—Arabic for hello. When she got no reply, she continued, 'We go to Tell Burak—visit AUB site, okay?' The soldier still said nothing and then waved them through.

After they continued, James said, 'Talkative aren't they?' as he put away his ID.

'Yes. Most are just kids, James, but the government owns the entire coast down here, so at least we get some protection from looting.' After a short drive, Natasha turned off the road, and they continued on a dirt track for the last part of their journey, which took them through a forest of banana trees, down to the coast. They drew up at a fence where a number of other cars were parked, close to a metal gate, which was already open. The site was an area of low grass, with the banana plantations growing on the land behind. In the middle was the tell, a low mound composed of the detrius of human habitation rising to a height of some twenty meters from the coastline. *Great*, thought James, *finally, we're alone at the end of the world.* Natasha turned and kissed James passionately on the mouth. With the engine stopped, the car was soon hot from the morning sun, and both of them were covered in perspiration. Suddenly, there was a tap on the car window, and a young man began speaking to them in German. James quickly released her from their embrace, and Natasha, still flushed, opened her door to greet one of the members of the dig team. She started to speak in German, but when James got out of the car, she introduced him as an old friend from Switzerland.

It appeared that the cost of the dig was being shared between the AUB and one of the universities in Germany, and excavation was shared between the two. The young German explained that they often come down to the site just before dawn to take advantage of the coolest hours of the day. Most of the students had already gone down to the shore for a swim, or to find some shade from the sun, but he was happy to show them around. Meanwhile, Natasha having discretely rearranging her skirt and adjusted her hair, they all moved off through the gate to make a tour of the site. As they walked up to the summit of the tell, their guide explained that there had been three periods of occupation at the tell: the Middle Bronze Age, the Iron Age, and the Islamic Medieval period. This was where they had found a large mud brick building dating to the Middle Bronze Age, with huge amounts of Earth piled up all around for protection. The building had served as a fortified stronghold on what was and still is a fertile coastal plain. A considerable number of finds had been made; both metal objects and pieces of cooking pots, storage jars, and a few imported Greek objects. However, the strangest object was a metal stele with just eight letters engraved on it. Natasha reached out for James's hand as they moved down to what was described as the medieval part of the site. In a loud voice, she said, 'James, this is what I was telling you about. This find is most unusual; maybe you can help us date it?' With the tour almost over, their guide nodded and pointed to a large tent where other members of the dig team were resting in the shade. 'Yes, why not,' he said, 'I'm sure we could all do with a cool drink in this heat.' And he led the party the shade of a large olive tree and a few bushes growing close to the shoreline, with tufts of spiky grass all around. The front was open to the sea, with one side held back to catch what little breeze there was. A number of rough wooden tables had been set in the centre to display the latest finds, and a couple of young students were resting on the rush-covered floor to one side. In the shade at the back was a small fridge, surrounded by a number of wooden chairs and a table with plastic cups and bottles of water. The small group of three settled down in the chairs to relax after the heat outside. James smiled at Natasha as their host opened the fridge and offered his guests a soft drink of fizzy orangeade, which they both accepted gratefully. After they settled down, James asked about the strange medieval object they had found. The German professor rose to his feet, went over to the display table, took a small object out of a box, and handed it to James. It appeared to be a metal stele, but much smaller than the big stones used to mark boundaries in the ancient Near East. It was like nothing James had seen before: a thin metal blade, eight to ten inches long, made of bronze with a circular handle at the top. On one side were engraved just eight letters: O.U.O.S.V.A.V.V in Roman text, framed by two letters, *D* and *M*, below. The reverse of the metal object was blank. Everyone looked at James for an explanation, as he cradled the object in his hand.

'So, if you found this in the medieval section of the dig, it may have come from the Beaufort Castle, not far from here,' said James. 'The castle was named by the Crusaders who occupied it in the twelfth century, referring to it in Arabic as 'Qasr al-Bofort.' This structure represents one of the few cases where a medieval castle proved of military value right up until the mid-twentieth century.' James was in full stride of his knowledge and added, 'T. E. Lawrence once described it as the finest medieval castle in the Arab world.' He spoke as if the opinion of the famous British army officer gave some credence to his report.

A reply came from the German straight and fast, 'Yes, but what does the inscription mean, and where was it made?'

James was surprised at his questions as Natasha came to his rescue, 'Probably a bit early for that now,' she said. 'Let me take it back to the AUB and see what we can find from our research there.' Everyone smiled and nodded at the solution, and the professor went to find a plastic bag to protect his valuable find. Whilst they waited, sand flies started to appear, and in the heat, they were most interested in the warm human bodies sitting still. Feeling impatient, James tapped the metal stele on the table beside him. Almost immediately, the metal emitted a deafening high-pitch note, and everyonepresent covered his ears in defence. 'Well,' said James, laughing; 'now we know this could be a kind of tuning fork. And, it can get rid of your flies, if nothing else!' The professor smiled at him, and taking the object, he placed it in a protective bag and gave it to Natasha. With that, they all stood up to shake hands before leaving the site at last.

James and Natasha walked back to the car in the bright sunlight. A small breeze had started to blow in from the sea, which gave some relief from the heat. Natasha opened the door of the car and, leaning inside, started the engine and put the air conditioner on full blast. James opened his door to get rid of the hot air inside, and they both stood looking at each other across the car roof. 'You were very coy back there, James. What do you really think about this stele thing?' She waved the object in her hand.

James looked at her and replied, 'I would be very careful with that, if I were you. It may be something that we don't understand. Tell me where exactly it was found and by whom.' His tone had gone serious.

'Well, from what I remember, it was discovered by our German guide on the floor of the Islamic house you saw, along with some Ottoman pipes. That would date the piece to between the seventeenth and eighteenth centuries. What about the strange inscription? Do you know what it means?' she asked.

'Come on,' said James, 'let's get inside and close the doors. The a/c must be working by now.' Natasha did as James suggested. As she sat down, she pulled up her long skirt to let the cool air blow between her legs. James could see she was just wearing her bikini underneath. He took the stele and looked again at the inscription through the plastic wrapper before commenting further. 'I'm sure this was made in Europe,' he observed, 'from the shape and workmanship of the engraved letters. But it's difficult to know what it means. In fact, with just eight letters and only the Roman inscription "D M" below, it's going to be difficult to decipher without more of the coded material. You're sure they found nothing more?' He looked at Natasha more closely. When she didn't answer, James put the object in the glove box and took out his map again. 'Right,' he said. 'Let's go and see if we can find this castle overlooking the Litani River, and we can eat our lunch on the way.' He pointed to the basket of food still sitting on the back seat. Natasha looked disappointed as the car moved back up the track through the banana trees again. 'Oh, James,' she said, 'I thought we might find somewhere quiet for lunch by the sea.' James saw the glint in her eye, but he was determined to find out what she was hiding from him.

As they drove back up to the main road and headed north towards Sidon, Natasha turned to James and explained there was a good road from Zahrani on the coast, which would take them up to the main town of Nabatiye. From there, they would have to find a way, if he wanted to see the Litani River. James took two apples from the basket and handed her one to eat as they drove along.

'So, James, what's your sudden interest in this northernmost part of the Great Rift Valley they call the Bekaa?' she asked. 'You know it's the longest fault in Lebanon and links the major fault of the Jordan valley to the Ghab Valley fault of Northern Syria. I went to some lectures on the geology of Lebanon, and it's really interesting.' James just smiled as she went on. 'The Lebanese segment of the Dead Sea fault originated some ten million years ago, as the boundary between the Arabian plate and the African plate, and has been moving ever since. Geologists have estimated that the Bekaa has moved almost 50 kilometres northwards since then with respect to Mount Lebanon, which hasn't moved at all!'

Amazing, thought James. *This girl has lived in the country for only a couple of years and already knows more than most who have spent their whole lives here.* He replied, 'As I'm sure you know, the Great Rift Valley runs roughly north to south for about 4,000 miles from Syria to central Mozambique in East Africa. Astronauts say it's the most significant feature on the planet visible from space. My interest,' said James 'is in the tectonics and whether this drove evolutionary changes, or whether climate and tectonics drove the changes separately. The formation of the Rift Valley, with its high mountains and lakes, caused big shifts in the global climate from very wet to very dry, and may have pushed our ancestors down the human path.'

Natasha looked at James and replied, 'Wow! You mean we're driving up this road to rock the cradle of humanity? Really, I like it.' And she shifted in her seat to pull her skirt up above her knees again. James could see that she was excited by his research and waited for what would come next. Fortunately, the traffic was light as the car started to climb up the road away from the coast, and finally they saw a signpost pointing to Nabatiye.

'Now listen to me, James,' said Natasha. 'From what I can remember from university, there are two long-held theories on this—the turnover theory and the variable selection theory. I think those were the names, but neither is capable of telling the whole story. About two million years ago, the El Nino currents increased to what they are now and may have caused more rapid climate change. This was at the time of the first appearance of *Homo erectus*, or modern man. But, at our university, we started to research orbital forcing … you know what I told you before. That's the wobble of the Earth on its axis of rotation around the sun. Geologists have known for years that orbital forcing controls the waxing and waning of ice ages, which affects tropical climates as well. Then, when the analysis of human DNA became possible, we realized that all humans on the planet today originate from just six family groups in Africa, and this is probably related to this extreme climate change. After that, the human race grew to what it is today. Really it's an amazing story of chance, and obviously, it's still going on.'

At this point, as they approached the outskirts of Nabatiye, James realized he wanted to stretch his legs and get a drink. 'Well if you ask me,' he said, 'modern man is still being driven by the search for food, so let's stop in the village and see if we can find some refreshments there.' Natasha pulled down her skirt again as the car approached the main street of Nabatiye at last.

Nabatiye, South Lebanon—Thursday, 29 June 2006

The road into the village was broken in places from years of poor repair, and suddenly James could see that the car was headed for a huge pothole on his side of the car. He franticly shouted a warning at Natasha, but at the same time, an old woman wearing a headscarf and carrying a bulky bag ran in front of their car. Natasha braked as hard as she could, and the car swerved to the left, but not before the front wheel hit the pothole. Along with the sickening jolt, came a deafening vibration from the glove box of the car.

James put his hands over his face and then covered his ears as the noise increased in velocity. Natasha threw herself towards James. They sat there motionless, while the old woman walked past in front of the vehicle. Then, as suddenly as it had started, the noise stopped, and in the silence, James realized the engine of the car had stalled. He slowly lowered his window and stretched to look outside. He could see the wheel was right on the edge of a very deep hole. Pushing Natasha back into her seat, he checked to make sure she was okay and said, 'I want you to start the engine and turn the wheel to the left and make a U-turn back down the road.' Natasha, pale white from the shock, nodded at him, and when the traffic was all clear, she turned the car around and pulled up on the other side of the road.

'James, what the hell, happened back there?' she whispered.

'Well, I think we were caught up in some sort of time slip, probably caused by that object in the glove box. But did you see how we also moved forward in time?' he replied.

'No, James, I was too terrified to see much at all, tell me what you saw.'

'When the old woman passed in front of the car, the road was full of rubble and abandoned cars. And the shops around us were broken and smashed, from what looked like military shelling,' he explained.

'But, James, that's just not possible. When do you think that happened?'

'That's the problem,' said James. 'I saw this scene on the front page of a French newspaper; the date was 17 July 2006—little more than two weeks from now. James opened the glove box and took out the metal object; it looked exactly as before, still wrapped and sealed in a plastic bag. 'Come on, I think it's time we made our way back to the coast, and we need to have a chat about this. Would you like me to drive?'

James drove back to the main coast road, after which they went north past Sidon towards Damour. At some point, Natasha told him to turn off at a junction and cross back over the highway. As they drove over the bridge, a column of Lebanese army trucks was on the highway below driving south. Natasha looked at James in alarm and said, 'Do you really think there is going to be a war?' James just nodded and drove on down towards the coast. Soon they were on a badly rutted, unmade road, driving slowly down through another plantation of banana trees. Natasha explained that this was where her family had a small house close to the sea. At the end of the track was a walled property with high metal gates, which were locked shut. 'That's strange.' said Natasha as James braked the car to a stop. 'These gates should be open.' She searched in her bag until she found a key. Leaving the car, she opened the gates for James, and he drove down a gravel driveway planted with new palm trees. James was quite impressed as he parked the car under the shade of the trees, but it was clear there was no one about. Looking at his watch, he noticed it was just after four in the afternoon, so he guessed that any workers had left for the day. Natasha was not so sure and ran around to the back of the house called out for the caretaker. Finally she returned to James. Pointing to an area beyond the backyard, she said, 'Would you go down there and see if anyone was working in the garden? I'll go and start the generator. If we don't water the new trees today, everything will soon be dead.' James wandered around the back, but no one was there, just some dark clouds over the sea to the west and bright sunshine overhead.

When James came back, he found that Natasha had taken off her skirt and blouse and was stripped down to a bikini. Her body had filled out, probably from childbirth, since her time in Switzerland, but she looked fit and still had an attractive figure. 'Here, James, I found these swimming shorts for you.' She passed him a pair of Bermuda shorts. 'You can get quite wet watering the trees, if you don't mind helping me? You can change in the servants' flat we made on the ground floor, there's no one there now.'

James looked at Natasha. 'What happened?' he asked.

'Well, I made a few calls and it seems all the farm workers left this morning for Damascus and may not be back for a while. I'll get the water pipes out from the shed over there, if you can join me when you're changed.' James nodded and smiled as he realized that the Syrians knew exactly what was going happen next and had fled. It was now only a question of how much time they had left.

James quickly changed in the small apartment, which was equipped with a shower, a small bed, and an air conditioning unit. When he went back outside, he found Natasha moving a number of large rubber hoses out to water the new palm trees. James noticed that her body was well tanned and could see strong muscles on both her arms and legs as she carried each heavy roll onto the driveway. On seeing James, she smiled at him and said, 'Hi there, can you start by connecting each hose to the stand pipes? I'll go and start the pump.' James had been watering gardens most of his life, but had not seen a system like this before. When he connected the hose to the pipe, the pressure of water shot out and gave him a good soaking. By the time Natasha returned, he was hot and covered in spray. She came to help him carrying a towel and laughing, until he sprayed her with water as well. In the hot weather, both of them were getting excited at being alone together. Natasha took the towel and, wiping his face, said, 'Thanks, James, now you can go and shower and I'll finish up out here.' Looking back at her figure again, he hoped it would not be long before she joined him.

James took a cold shower, which was most refreshing after the heat outside. He was washing his hair when there was a tap at the glass door, and the next minute she was naked under the shower with him. The look in her eyes told him she was in heat. He roughly pushed his fingers inside her and tried to lift her up, but the space was too confined to raise her legs. Instead, he carried her out of the shower, their mouths locked together, as he tried to enter her again. As they staggered across the room entwined together, she murmured in his ear, 'It's all right. I've locked the door. You can do what you want with me.' What she didn't mention was that she had brought the metal object from the car and placed it under the covers. As he laid her down on the small bed, her hand reached out and grasped the steel. Needing no further invitation, he knelt down and spread himself upon her open thighs, her body musk exciting him further. Suddenly, they both stopped as strong vibrations shook the room. They were cast back in time to the grasslands in Africa a million years ago! A hot wind was blowing through the long grass, and he could see distant thunderclouds over high mountains. He had an unstoppable instinct to mate with the female below him. He was fighting her now, shaking her head in his hands as he sank himself deep into her and took possession of his mate at last. The figure below him was also aroused with almost animal excitement, causing her to cry out as she could not stop the orgasm that was building within her. In another moment, he emptied his hot liquid inside her. As he did, his mate below was making loud cries, which were being answered by the animals around them. He raised his head in fear of what their sounds might attract and pressed his fingers into her mouth to silence her. Finally, she was engulfed by a stronger climax, which left her quite unconscious for a time. Slowly, the mists cleared, and with their primordial coupling over, James at last withdrew from her. He slowly took the metal stele from her hand and placed it on the floor under the bed, wondering if she had known what might happen. Moving slowly to the far side of her, he felt exhausted. He ran his fingers through her damp hair and then fell asleep with the sound of African animals ringing in his ears.

When James awoke he was alone on the bed and felt cold. Natasha must have turned up the air conditioner and got dressed already. James sighed when he saw that the metal object under the bed was also gone. *Women,* he thought, *often two steps ahead of men in some things and one step behind in others.* He showered quickly and got dressed in his slacks and T-shirt again. Once outside, he found Natasha loading up the car with what looked like personal items. 'James!' she exclaimed. 'Or should I say Mr Tarzan! Darling, you were wonderful. Just what I needed today.' She approached him and hugged him, rubbing her hand against his pants again. She had changed back into her long skirt and a new top, but her face was still flushed, and she was wearing a scarf to cover up marks on her neck.

'Natasha, really, that was like being in a zoo, but I'm glad you enjoyed it. How did you know we would go back in time like that?' demanded James. He tried to sound serious, but after what they had done together, he knew she would still be charged up with a lot of emotion.

'Well, I didn't, but I thought, if you could go forward in time, maybe it could help me go back to satisfy my needs as well. Don't you know it gets pretty difficult for a woman at times, so I guess this thing can help you go back or forward in time, whichever way you want. At least that's what Deepak said.'

James looked at her in amazement, as now it was clear who was behind this affair. James took Natasha in his arms. 'And what, exactly, did Deepak propose?' he asked her.

'Well, not a lot really,' she answered. 'Just that you would contact me in Beirut, and that we have to take the stele to the Temple of Jupiter in Baalbek. Have you ever been to the opening night? It's on Wednesday, 12 July, this year.'

James just looked at her again and kissed her fully on the mouth, so that her passion was rekindled again. 'Yes,' he said, coming up for air, 'by some strange chance, we have been invited by a client, but after what we've seen today, I'm not sure if the international festival will even take place this year. If the events in Nabatiye were from around 16 July, then I'm thinking maybe we should change our flights and leave Beirut early next week.

Natasha looked at James in horror. 'That's just not possible, James, is it?'

To which he replied, 'With all the extreme political groups around here, anything is possible, and it will almost certainly start in the south. Look, it's past six in the evening. Can we discuss this in the car, if you're ready?'

Natasha closed up the house. They got in the car and drove through the gates. After Natasha got out and locked the gates, she carefully drove back to the main highway and on towards Beirut. As they headed back, James thought hard about what to do next, but finally it was Natasha who made a suggestion. 'What if I were to invite you to stay for the weekend, and we somehow find the time to visit Baalbek one evening?'

'Sounds good to me,' said James. 'It may be the last opportunity to go there for a while.'

Temple of Jupiter, Baalbek, Bekaa Valley, Lebanon—Saturday, 1 July 2006

The Nissan Land Cruiser was descending onto the main road from the pass through Mount Lebanon down onto the Bekaa valley. The temperature gauge in the SUV started to go up from below 30 degrees Celsius at the top of the pass. By the time they reached the first town of Chtaura, Lebanon, it had risen to almost 35 degrees. James thought it was going to be a hot evening. They had left Natasha's house in the mountains just before five in the afternoon, on the dubious pretext of going to a music rehearsal for the forthcoming international concert in Baalbek. The weather was cool in the mountains, and no one else at the house wanted to brave the evening heat at Baalbek. James had offered to accompany her so she would not be alone, in what was the spiritual home of Hezbollah—the Lebanese political and military organisation, the Party of God.

Natasha turned up the air conditioning a notch and drove carefully as the big car ate up the miles on the dusty road. Over black slacks, she was wearing a silver-embroidered top that fully covered her. She also was wearing a dark headscarf around her neck. James was dressed in dark trousers, a red T-shirt, and a blue summer jacket. They were aiming at looking like ordinary tourists. As they came to a number of new roundabouts on the highway, James saw a sign for Zahle. This was the last Christian town in the Bekaa Valley, before they entered Hezbollah territory. James looked at Natasha. 'Look, why not make a detour to Zahle and have dinner at the Grand Hotel?' he suggested sheepishly.

'James, my dear, we have a meeting with Deepak, in case you've forgotten,' she replied. 'He is expecting us to deliver the stele, which is carefully packed in the wooden box between us.' Natasha raised the armrest between them to show James where she had hidden the mysterious object.

'Okay then, let's press on to the end,' he replied.

Shortly after the next turning, they entered the final straight road leading to Baalbek where yellow flags of the political wing of Hezbollah had been placed on every electrical pylon as a welcome to the expected visitors. James watched in anticipation as the sun started to go down behind the mountains to the west. The land was flat, and there were only a few houses. Most of the grass was dried brown by the hot summer sunshine. There was little evidence of any irrigation or agriculture. As they approached the town of Baalbek, the yellow flags were replaced by the black flags of the military wing of Hezbollah and large posters of the Muslim leaders of the party. Natasha could see that James was starting to look worried, and she patted his knee in reassurance as they entered the town of Baalbek and looked for directions to the archaeological site. 'From my last visit, I remember a car park we can use, right in front of the entrance. It should only be a short walk to the Temple of Bacchus for this musical rehearsal.' Natasha looked at the advance programme she held in her hand. 'Well, it should be the Salzburg Chamber Soloists, and if you are interested, they will be playing Haydn, Symphony No.

49, 'La Passione' this year. Should be right up your street, James.' Natasha took the small wooden box, and when they opened the doors of the car, they were hit by the hot evening air. James said nothing and followed her across the car park just as the last tourist coach was leaving. He took her hand as they crossed the road and walked towards the entrance, now overshadowed by the foreboding stone building. With darkness quickly approaching, James looked up at the night sky and could make out the planet Venus in retrograde motion, as the evening star. He had not seen the sky as clear as this since his time at sea.

There was no one at the entrance, just a well-worn hole in the hedge and a broken metal fence, so they followed the path towards the dark shape of the best-preserved Roman Temple in the world. This huge monument, often referred to as the 'Temple of the Sun', was almost complete, surrounded by forty-two columns, each nearly twenty meters high. As they approached, they saw that a gaslight had been placed on a chair on the steps, and two bodyguards in Arab headdress were standing watch. No music could be heard at all. Natasha pulled the scarf over her head as they approached the two men. Both she and James were now more fearful of their situation.

'*As-salaam alaykum.*' Natasha spoke as a more formal greeting in Arabic. The two men looked at them both suspiciously and said nothing. '*Tatakullum Inggleezi?*' she went on, asking if they spoke any English. She waved the music programme at the men. By now, James could see inside the temple. He suddenly realized that this was no music rehearsal, but some political meeting. He could see a large audience and Hezbollah and Lebanese flags placed against the walls. On the stage addressing the seated crowd was one of the mullahs James had seen on the posters, with a black beard, although he thought they all looked the same. It was quite obvious he and Natasha had blundered in on something where they would not be welcome.

At last a man with smooth black hair and dressed in a suit and a tie came to their rescue. 'I'm sorry, but this temple is closed tonight. We will be saying evening prayers shortly. Perhaps you would like to look at the Temple of Jupiter over there before you leave?'

James nodded and apologized, 'Sorry for the intrusion.' He turned to Natasha, 'Come along, darling, there's a lot more to see over there.' And he pointed to the six standing columns of the Temple of Jupiter, now silhouetted against the night sky.

But Natasha was having none of it and started to argue with the man. 'Look we arranged to come and meet here with this music group, so what exactly is going on tonight?'

Just as James was turning to leave, the man looked at Natasha more closely. He pulled down her scarf and realized he had seen her before. 'Wait!' he shouted. 'You're not tourists! You're that Russian scientist from the AUB. I've seen you here before. Tell me, who exactly is this friend?' he asked of Natasha directly.

'This is Professor Pollack from Switzerland,' replied Natasha coolly. 'He is here to meet with a colleague of ours.'

'That would be the strange Indian man over by your dig, would it?' he went on. 'So, we appear to have two meetings here tonight at the same time, both of them most private.' He smiled at her knowingly as the meeting inside erupted into shouts of applause. 'Well it sounds as if the international festival is going to be delayed this year. Very soon any tourist will be most unwise to visit this site,' he explained.

'Yes,' Natalie replied. 'From what we have seen, we had better close down the dig tonight.' Unconsciously, she tapped the wooden box in her hands. James looked in horror at the box, but nothing happened.

'I can send you some men to close up the entrance when you have finished,' the man offered. And, with that, he left them standing on the steps with the two guards. Natalie looked at the men and muttered '*Ma'asalaama*,' but got no reply. As she turned away to leave, she was almost in tears. 'So bloody close,' she exclaimed. 'This is the greatest discovery since Christ, and it is stopped by a stupid war. Why, James? Why is it always like this in my life?'

James looked at her as they walked slowly down the main entrance towards the largest temple of all, the Temple of Jupiter, which was glowing in the soft moonlight. 'All right,' he said at last. 'Tell me exactly what you have found here.'

'We have known for some time there's a tell under the Roman Jupiter temple. It dates back over 9,000 years. You realize that's *seven thousand years* before Christ! We started to question who built the foundations.'

'So, if the Roman's didn't put the stones in place, who did?' asked James.

'That's exactly what we have been trying to establish,' replied Natasha. 'Look I'm not saying people couldn't have done it, I'm just wondering how they could have done it! The walls here are built of over twenty monoliths, each weighing 300 tons. On the western side, there is a retaining wall of three stones—they form a trilithon—each estimated to weigh over 750 tons. Now you tell me how they moved these huge blocks of stone from the quarry over a mile away.'

As they turned the corner and came closer to the temple, James looked at the huge blocks set in the wall. 'Yes, I read about that, but wasn't it thought possible that they might have flipped the big stones over and over again to move them?'

'Right,' replied Natasha. 'That has been done on a small scale, but never with stones the size of the largest stones here. Really, James, we couldn't move these blocks with modern machinery today!'

'Well, someone did it,' replied James. As they rounded the next corner of the temple, they could see a green tent had been placed against the wall, just below one the largest trilithon—a configuration of three massive rocks. It was roped off with red-and-white boards. James assumed that the signs in Arabic said 'No Entry'. Sitting inside the tent beneath an electric light was Deepak, still wearing his overcoat, and waiting for them.

'Ah, there you two are, and about time!' he said by way of greeting. 'I was getting worried. Now you both know there is going to be a little local disturbance around here, so we need to close off all the excavations you have done below.' He got up and began moving around. 'Well, we can't have these people suddenly appearing in Babylon, or worse still at the temple in Jerusalem! That would cause even more problems.' He turned to Natasha. 'So James and I will go down and close the stones below if you can replace all the excavations on the surface, all right, Natasha?' he ordered briskly.

'Okay, but how are you going to get out from underneath the foundations?' she asked.

'Don't worry. James and I are only going to go on a short trip. Now give me the box with the stele. We have a lot of work to do.' Natasha handed Deepak the wooden box. Taking out the metal object, he placed it inside his coat. 'Right, James,' he said. 'Come along. We need to be in Rome by the morning.' And with that, he disappeared into the darkness below.

Natasha looked at James and embraced him, tears running down her cheeks. 'I hate it when you leave like this with Deepak. You will come back and see me when this is all over, won't you?' And, giving him a quick kiss, she hurried off into the night.

James entered the tent and descended a ladder to the next level below. It was necessary to squeeze through a small opening just below a huge trilithon. Deepak was waiting inside the temple. The underground chamber was lit by a string of small lights where excavation had been done to expose another level below. They were standing in a huge stone cavern with the monoliths above and a stone floor below.

Only now Deepak explained, 'The people who built this were clever. They used these big stones to prevent access from the outside, so the temple can only be opened from inside. Watch carefully as we start the closure process.' With a grinding noise, a huge megalith started to move back into place below the trilithon stone above, sealing the entrance from visitors again. James watched in wonder as the huge stone fell back into place, effectively trapping them inside. 'Now come along, James,' said the guardian, 'we need to move on from here.' Then Deepak made his way towards an opening in the floor. James could see that someone had excavated a hole in the floor that gave access to the level below. With the help of the lights, he could just make out a small flight of stone steps descending into the darkness. On descending down there, in the centre of the floor was a rush mat of the type found in Egypt. As Deepak moved the mat to one side, James saw it had concealed a raised circular opening. Looking into the opening, James saw the wormhole. Suddenly, a bright yellow glow and flashes of bright light filled the chamber. James wondered exactly where they were going this time. Finally, Deepak set the pendant around his neck to their destination. 'Rome,' said Deepak. 'Now then, we need a special date in July for this to work. Let's move to a good saints day, Sunday, 16 July 2006. Looks as if it might be possible, at around ten a.m., to meet both Alexei and Natasha.' James shuddered at the thought of 16 July, but was intrigued to hear the mention of the two names. 'Right, ready, James.' And with that, they clung together and jumped into the wormhole.

Church of San Lorenzo in Lucina, Rome—Sunday, 16 July 2006

James awoke sitting outside at a table in a street-side café somewhere in Rome. The morning sun was already shining brightly, but under the sunshade it was still cool. Sitting opposite him at the metal table was Deepak, still wearing his black overcoat. James slumped forward on the table and said, 'Deepak, do you know where we are? I thought you were taking me somewhere important this time, like the Sistine Chapel!'

Deepak looked at him with despair, 'Actually, I thought that went rather well. Here you are in one piece sitting at a table in the sunshine! You never know about these pavement cafe's, if they'll be open or closed for the summer—with all the tables and chairs removed, see!' he replied.

'Okay, but where exactly are we?' James asked again.

'Well, we are sitting just off the square of San Lorenzo, and over there is the church of San Lorenzo in Lucina, an ancient parish church. It was rebuilt in the twelfth century and dedicated to St. Lawrence, with just a minor basilica for Rome.' He pointed across the square to the church, which had six columns visible outside.

'Right, yes I can see it,' said James, 'but what's so special about this place?'

'All in good time. You should appreciate the calm of Rome on a Sunday morning ... the smell of Italian coffee,' said Deepak. 'Ah! Here it comes now. I ordered you a cappuccino, if that's all right?' Deepak replied, as a waiter placed two large cups of white froth on the table.

But James was looking in amazement up the street at someone who was approaching the square. Walking towards him, dressed in a white blouse and black skirt, was Alexei, or at least someone who looked just like her. James paused for just a moment, but then got up from his chair. As he did, she noticed him as well.

'James, it is you? I can't believe it! What are you doing here in Rome?' she asked as James approached. Placing his arms on her shoulders, he gave her a kiss on each cheek. Before he could answer, she saw his companion. 'Oh! I see you're with your Indian friend again.' She pointed towards Deepak.

'Ah, yes,' James replied. 'Well, I think we've come to see the church here.'

'I hope so,' she said. 'You're just in time for the morning mass. Shall I see you inside when you've finished your coffee?'

James looked towards Deepak, who nodded and then replied, 'Yes, of course, see you inside.'

James was wondering what was going on, as Alexei started to walk across the square towards the church of San Lorenzo. When James sat down, he looked across at Deepak, smiled, and said, 'You knew she would be here, didn't you? I suppose Nathalie is waiting inside the church. Is that what we came for?' he asked urgently. 'Is one of those two getting married, and this is a way to get me to be there? Well it can't be Alexei, or she would have said something. So it must be something to do with Nathalie. Is that it, Deepak?' By now James was getting excited.

'No, James, it's not quite like that. Now drink your coffee, and I'll explain on the way.' As soon as he finished speaking, the five-minute bell started to chime to remind the faithful of the service. James and Deepak both rose from the table and walked across the square towards the six columns at the church entrance. When they reached the iron railings between the pillars, Deepak stopped and spoke to James. 'I'm afraid this is as far as I can go. You see, James, you must decide the next step in your life, right here, right now.' James looked puzzled as Deepak went on, 'Yes, it does concern Nathalie, but the decision to go with her has to be yours.' With that, he reached into his coat pocket and took out the stele he had been given at the temple in Baalbek. 'Nathalie wants to join her mother in the future with the help of this.' He held out the metal object to James. 'We have come to this church in Rome because this is where Poussin is buried. Inside this church is a monument with the four shepherds, the tomb, and the Latin inscription 'Et in Arcadia Ego'. Nathalie thinks it may be possible to move forward through the tomb from here, but it will be dangerous. She wants to give you the opportunity to come with her and join her mother, no?'

In the last ten seconds, James's life had crumbled into dust. 'James, you have helped Nathalie by doing what she asked by finding this special object. That goes some way towards redemption, but the final decision is yours.'

James thought fast and replied, 'You said it would be dangerous, can you explain why?'

Deepak explained, 'Going forward from here could harm the church, so best if I stay outside to keep everything together.'

'Right, and is there no other solution?' asked James quickly.

'Well, yes,' said Deepak, 'it might be possible, if you go back to Beirut at the same time! Equal and opposite forces may cancel each other out. Butthe time travel wouldhave to be done at precisely the same time!'

James smiled at him. 'All right, let's do it, if you think there's a chance,' he replied.

With that, Deepak handed James the stele and, taking the medallion in his hand, thought for a moment. 'This is going to be difficult. We need to find the time of day you last saw Natasha before you left Beirut.'

Now it was James who had to think, 'Really how can I know that? I haven't lived it yet! Except we were planning to invite them all to the yacht club in Jounieh next week, maybe Wednesday or Thursday, but I can't be sure,' he replied in desperation.

'Right,' said Deepak, 'let's try Wednesday, 5 July, at ... say around 11.00 a.m. outside the security gate. That should be possible.' Having set the time and date, Deepak inserted the stele into the medallion and then gave it back to James. 'Now listen, James, I may not see you again for a while. When you enter the church, it's the second chapel on the right-hand side. You should find Nathalie at the tomb.' James and Deepak embraced each other and, as James entered the portico of the church, Deepak shouted after him, pointing at a poster, 'James, look, there's a visiting choir from Sofia at this morning's service!' And then Deepak waved him good-bye.

James opened the heavy wooden door and entered the church where the service had already started. The white arches in the nave were decorated with bright figures, while above the ceiling was a series of gold squares. A painting of Christ looked down on the congregation. High above the altar, a painting of the crucifixion hung between six black marble pillars, over which hung a golden sun. The small group of singers was seated below the altar on the left, as James quietly made his way towards the chapel on the right. He could see the white marble monument engraved with a reproduction of the four shepherds of Arcadia and the inscription 'Even in Arcadia I exist' as if spoken by death itself. Beneath the bust of Poussin was written in French: 'From Chateaubriand to Nicholas Poussin, for the glory of the arts and the honour of France'. *So this was in fact a gift from the well-known writer Victor Hugo*, thought James. The big question however, was why Chateaubriand should have chosen the Arcadian shepherds for his memorial, out of so many paintings by Poussin. As James turned into the small chapel, he saw there kneeling at the altar tomb of Poussin was Nathalie, wearing a pure white cotton dress with a bright red silk sash around her waist. Standing at the back, and now holding a posy of flowers, was Alexei, with tears running down her face. No one in the small group moved. It was as if time itself had stopped. Finally, there was a muffled sound from the choir as they stood to sing. As James listened to the words, he realized the chant was familiar tune to him, and looked for an explanation from Alexei. Finally she approached and came next to him, whispered in his ear, 'This is a type of Gregorian chant, which Nathalie likes very much in her home country. Some of the words are based on the beliefs of the old French Christian sect, the Cathars,' she explained. 'You see, James, after you left me, I had a disastrous marriage and became attracted to other woman. Then I met Nathalie, and we have become lovers. I have to admit she is very beautiful today.'

James winced at the explanation then nodded, as if accepting the news. 'You can't translate any of this song, can you?' he asked.

'Actually the Latin words do have a meaning, but this chant is about stones. Roughly in English it says: "Take me to the inside, absorb, and take me." I really don't understand the meaning.'

But James was not so sure. 'Is there such a place in Italy?

'Yes, there is a town called Lecco in the Gulf of Naples. The name probably comes from the Greek word *petra*, meaning "stone" if that's any help,' she replied.

'Thanks, Alexei, that may explain a number of things. Let's see what happens next.' And they stood by to wait for Nathalie to make her decision.

The singing continued louder as the choir reached the chorus of the chant, and then, as they sang the last line, Nathalie stood up and turned to face James. He held the stele out to her and smiled. 'Now, you're absolutely sure about this then?'

She nodded and replied, 'And you, James, what did you decide?'

'Yes, of course, but if you go forward in time, I need to go back in time, or you may damage the frescos around here.'With that she took the stele and plunged it into the marble at the heart of the tomb. At first, her hand completely disappeared into solid stone, and then the tomb lit up as the object started to emit a high-pitched noise followed by a loud vibration. In a split second, the noise and vibrations absorbed her body and that of James. They both disappeared at the same time. Then the noise stopped almost as fast as it had started, leaving the chapel empty except for Alexei. Finally, the stone of the tomb ejected the stele, which fell onto the stone floor with a clatter, and the small chapel was silent again. In the meantime, the choir began another chant, and the service continued as if nothing had happened. Deepak had been right: the equal and opposite forces had cancelled each other out. Alexei bent down and picked up the stele, then she walked out of the church to see if James's Indian friend was still outside the church.

Jounieh bay, Lebanon—Wednesday, 6 July 2006

When James awoke this time, he was resting up against some iron railings, close to the sea, and a short distance from the entrance to a yacht club. He was sitting on dry grass by the side of the road. There was a bright blue sky, and a hot wind was blowing from the south. James knew he was outside the ATCL Club and back in Lebanon, just as Deepak had promised. He could hear the sound of the boats' halyards rattling against the masts in the wind and he could smell of the waves as they broke against the breakwater opposite him. It took him some minutes to recover all his senses. He had a bad headache, and his body felt compressed from the journey. James looked at his watch and saw it had stopped at exactly five minutes to eleven, which he thought was odd. Deepak was never early in these time transfers. He then saw that he was wearing his shorts and his favourite beach shirt. He also saw that a drop of blood had trickled from his nose and landed on his knee. He felt in his pocket for a handkerchief, but could find only some invitation papers. Wiping his nose on his forearm, he stood up at last and could see the gatehouse of the club, where security guards were checking the members' cars at the entrance. Slowly, he walked down to the shade offered by the building and waited, but could not remember what for. A few minutes passed, and then a Land Cruiser approached, which he knew very well. The car stopped at the barrier, near to where he was standing, and Natasha opened her door, just as James was about to collapse onto the road. She managed to open the back door just in time, and helped James climb onto the rear seat, next to her son.

The guard by now was asking to see the invitation tickets for the visitors. James felt in the pocket of his shorts and handed the tickets to Natasha. He smiled at her and, holding his head in his hands, said nothing. 'Don't talk now,' she said. 'Everything's going to be fine. I managed to change your air tickets for a flight out of here this Friday.'

With that, James spoke at last and slowly replied, 'I think there's something wrong with the time here.' Then he closed his eyes.

Natasha looked at him in surprise. 'You've noticed as well?' she asked. James nodded and pointed to his watch as Natasha went on. 'I had a call from Moscow this morning. It seems the Earth's rotation is slowing down, faster than expected!' Then she bent down and whispered in his ear, 'Let's get you down to the club. You can recover inside.'

They parked the car on the quay in front of the yachts, and James went inside to find somewhere to sit down out of the heat. The children quickly went off to find a place where they could swim, so that, by the time James re-joined the group, everyone was swimming at the entrance to the harbour. Shortly after noon, the boys wanted to eat, so his wife took them back to the club restaurant, leaving Natasha in the water. James lay on a sun bed watching the powerboats entering and leaving the harbour.

When he was finally alone, Natasha quickly climbed out of the water and came over to James. She was wearing a brown striped bikini, and the salt water glistened on her tanned body in the sun. She took a beach towel to dry her wet hair and sat down next to him. 'Now, James, tell me what happened!' she asked urgently.

'Well,' he replied thoughtfully, 'Natalie used the stele to go somewhere in the future, and I came back here. It was almost as simple as that, not including the headache. Actually I think that thing is dangerous. I did some research online before we went up to Baalbek, and it appears the letters are the same as the inscription on an Arcadian monument in England. It appears that no one has been able to decode the meaning,' he explained.

'So what does our great James think it could mean?' she asked.

'Yes, that's the interesting part. The owner of this stately home in England was a mason, so he may have had some common interest with the second Arcadian painting of Poussin. This implies that the tomb he painted contained some important Biblical figure, and some think it may have been Mary Magdalene!' he proposed. 'There's a clear message at the church in Rome. Something about "In this tomb

Poussin lives" and then it went on about how he lives and speaks in his paintings,' really quite strange.

'So you think Poussin was a Grand Master of the Knights Templar,' she asked.

'Well he lived in the seventeenth century, so he probably had access to the stories about the Knights Templers from the crusades,' he added.

'Yes, but weren't they persecuted for worshipping a godhead called Baphomet?' Natasha asked.

'Right, but that was the problem. This image worshipwas an old Gnostic rite involving the inner balancing of the masculine and feminine energies, which the church could not accept. Poussin's spiritual mentor was a Jesuit—Athanasius Kircher—one of the most learned Egyptologists at that time, who had knowledge of the stars and these old secrets,' he explained. 'You know that the Latin phrase Poussin painted—Et in arcadia ego—has been suggested as an anagram for 'I Tego arcano Dei.' Roughly translated it states "Begone—I conceal the secrets of God", but that's guesswork to me.'

'Well, James what's your best guess at this secret?' Natasha enquired.

'That's really difficult,' he replied. 'The Templers may have heard of the early Gnostic gospels of the Christian story, like the Gospel of Mary ... Mary Magdalene, the companion of Jesus. You can find it in all the bookstores here in Beirut.'

'So why won't the church admit these earlier gospels, which were excluded from the Bible?'

'Maybe they will, as religious ideas change,' he replied. 'The first group of disciples included a number of women, which for a lot of people is an important part of the story. This painting of the shepherds at a tomb may refer to the fall of the Mother Goddess in early Christian times and the end of the bridal chamber rite, sometimes referred to as the great divorce. There is a case that Jesus advocated this sacrament to unite men and women on an equal footing. Some think we live in a time when the old traditions of Christianity are dead, so that the light of civilization that came out of a Christian Europe, is flickering towards a new age of darkness,' he offered as an explanation.

Natasha stood up, preparing to leave. 'I suppose that would become a lot more controversial should women hold a position in the Church? Come on, let's go and join the children for lunch.'

But James stopped her. He wanted to hear more about his suspicions over the difference in time. 'Wait, tell me what you think about the Earth's slowing rotation,' he asked.

'Oh that,' she said. 'It's being going on for four and a half billion years. This slow change is very powerful and causes earthquakes and volcanoes to erupt from the changing stress on the Earth's crust. It's just starting to affect the planet more. The Asian tsunami in 2004, for example. As the Earth slows down, the oceans move towards the poles dragging the atmosphere with them, which can only increase climate change. If a really large volcano should explode, we might soon be into another ice age! She explained.

'Alright then, let's enjoy our life while we can,' he replied.

Epilogue—Days of discovery

Gland, Switzerland—Thursday 21 February 2010

He was sitting at the window looking at the snow melting on the bare plain trees outside on the terrace. It was almost four in the afternoon, and the sun was just setting in the west behind a group of tall fir trees. February had been cold this year, with regular snowfalls and a cold east wind. He was now a patient at a Swiss Clinique doing rehab after his operation. The days were full of physical activities to help repair his heart, and the nights were full of sleeplessness from the pain. He was waiting for his visitor in a large conservatory, complete with beige leather armchairs placed around low coffee tables. In front of him, he could just make out the lake, with the mountains behind covered in cloud.

At last his visitor arrived—a tall Englishman dressed in warm corduroy trousers and a casual pullover. He was not wearing his badge of office, but was well known to him as his chaplain. It was now after four, and he ordered a pot of tea for the two of them. The conversation at first was strained, but his vicar knew from experience how to make people relax. 'Do you want to tell me how you feel? Or shall we do that a little later?' asked the chaplain, sipping his tea.

'No, I'm much better now, it's just the trauma from the operation that worries me.' he replied. 'They've offered me a treatment called EMDR, which helps to remove bad memories and the stress after an operation,' he explained, looking out of the window.

'Really, do they know how that works?'

'I think the therapy mimics rapid eye movement during sleep. It's this movement that helps us move our traumatic memories into storage at the back of our brains.'

'You mean something like defragmentation on a computer? I think you must have had quite an experience at the hospital!'

'Yes, it was quite an experience. My heart was stopped for over an hour, which is needed for a repair. But it's really strange being out of your body. Recent research has found that the heart also has intelligence like the brain, more than half of it is composed of neurons, which pulsate and produce a strong electromagnetic signal, so you can guess what it feels like when it suddenly stops,' he explained.'The real problem is, I'm not really sure why I came back,' he continued.

'It all sounds most confusing, can you tell me what you saw?' asked his chaplain.

'Well, first it's very black ... not dark, but like a black void. Then I saw two small threads of light, one white and very bright, the other full of colour. There appeared to be no time or feeling there. Do you know where this place is? I think I chose the colours and came back here. Although it could have been just a bad dream,' he offered.

'Well, no one can tell you why you went there,' said the chaplain. 'But of course you came back. You went to hospital for a heart repair and not to die. That's what you and all the doctors planned, wasn't it?Look, choosing your life was the most important thing you have done. Now you have a second chance to do something different.' The chaplain's speech was calm.

'All right, so I came back to do what differently?' he asked again.

'I think you do what you do best ... perhaps helping other people, for example. You need to find another way ... perhaps a better way.' That was the best advice the chaplain could offer.'Now tell me about the novel you were writing the last time we meet. I read the draft you sent me. Interesting idea about this Arcadian monument in England. Have you done any more research?' asked his visitor.

'Yes, I've been able to correct some of the chapters in my spare time here, and I found a bit more about that strange inscription. Some years ago, the BBC made a documentary about the inscription and even got code breakers from Bletchley Park in England to try and decipher it. They thought that no code of ten letters was possible to break, so I thought I had drawn a blank,' he replied.

'You mean the inscription on the monument in England?' asked the chaplain looking surprised.

'Why, yes. It was commissioned in 1748 and paid for by Lord Anson. It features a carved image of the Nicholas Poussin painting of the shepherds, with those eight letters and *D M* inscribed below. Then I found a bizarre solution online from someone in Norway. He used the letters *D* and *M* as a key, and the Norwegian alphabet. His solution was that it reads "That was I Joshua".'

'Meaning that Jesus is the shepherd to humankind?' asked his visitor.

'No, the letters *D M* imply this was a memorial to the divine dead. In Latin it stands for "Dis Manibus", a common inscription on Roman tombstones. Is it possible thatthis refers to the tomb of Mary Magdalene and some early rite of the heart?' he asked. 'I have been reading here that Jesus wanted to restore the authority of the feminine principle—you know some sort of equality of man and woman in the contract of marriage. We have a good library here, and I found there was a rite in the past known as the sacrament of the bridalchamber which joined together the male and female energies,' he explained. 'I suppose you are going to tell me that there's milk for babies and meat for the men,' was all he answered.

'Yes, well it looks as if you are well on the way to a good recovery,' said the Chaplain. 'Now if you don't mind, I'm afraid it's almost time for me to leave.' They stood up, shook hands, and he was left alone. Looking outside, he knew it was going to be another cold and starry night.

THE END

Acknowledgements

The author is indebted to the following authors and their books:

- John Fowles, *Mantissa*, 1982.

- Glenn Beck, *An Inconvenient Book: Real Solutions to the World's Biggest Problems*, 2007

- George Bernard Shaw, *Arms and the Man*, 1894

- Steven Hawking, *Black Holes and Baby Universes and Other Essays*, 1994

- Alan Block and Constance Weaver, *All is clouded by De$ire: Global Banking, Money Laundering, and International Organized Crime*, 2004

- G. Edward Griffin, *The Creature from Jekyll Island*, 1994

- Marvin Meyer with Esther A. De Boer, *The Gospels of Mary: The Secret Tradition of Mary Magdalene, the Companion of Jesus*, 2004

- Victoria LePage, *Mysteries of the Bridechamber: The Initiation of Jesus and the Temple of Solomon*, 2007

The author is also indebted to the following organisations:

- Clinic for Cardiovascular Surgery,University Hospital of Geneva, Geneva, Switzerland

- CERN, the European Organisation for Nuclear Research, Geneva, Switzerland

- SLAC National Accelerator Laboratory, Menlo Park, California, U.S.A

- American University of Beirut, History and Archaeology Department, Beirut, Lebanon

- Clinique La Lignière, Gland, Switzerland

With additional thanks to D. H. Lawrence and his desk at school

Lightning Source UK Ltd.
Milton Keynes UK
UKOW050613161011

180374UK00002B/13/P